online catalogue. Fin
will include
of items

IN MEMORIAM

John McGahern (1934 – 2006)

'These are our lives. I can't get over it.'

—Maeve Brennan in a note to her *New Yorker* editor and colleague, William Maxwell.

Contents

by way of an introduction

A BOOK, A MAGAZINE, this object you are holding is both at once: an anthology of twenty-two new short stories, the twenty-second issue of *The Stinging Fly* literary magazine.

The magazine was established in 1997, we published our first issue in March 1998, and for the purposes of this introduction (and as a reminder for myself as much as for anyone else) it is worth including our mission statement here:

> *The Stinging Fly* was established to publish and promote new Irish and international writing. The editors recognise the need to provide a forum for new and emerging writers, particularly writers of fiction.
>
> The Stinging Fly's main objectives are:
> —To provide a forum for new Irish and international writing;
> —To foster new writing talent;
> —To present new writing in an attractive, high quality publication at an affordable price;
> —To introduce this new writing to as wide an audience as possible.

I have to be honest and admit that the thought of writing a mission statement hadn't entered my head, until asked to provide one, in one hundred words or less, with our first application to the Arts Council for annual funding. By then I was working on the third issue of the magazine—high time for me to stop and think about what it is I was setting out to do. Yet, even though they had not been formulated, the objectives were there from the beginning, and the work ever since has been an attempt to achieve them.

This anthology, although it does not come in the magazine's regular format, remains true to its spirit. *These Are Our Lives* gathers together twenty-two new short stories from twenty-two writers. Nearly all the work came into us via open submissions—from the stuffed, expectant envelopes sent to our PO Box on James's Street earlier this year. The writers are mostly, but not all, from Ireland. You will have heard of some of them before, but a good number of them are just beginning to publish.

I am happy that the anthology includes writers we've already featured in previous issues. It is a source of great pleasure to see new stories come in from writers such as Kevin Barry, Maria Behan, Jennifer Brady, David Butler, D.W. Lewis, Nuala Ní Chonchúir, Philip Ó Ceallaigh, Mary O'Donoghue, Aiden O'Reilly and Kevin Power, and to witness their work develop over time.

More satisfying still is the fact that the submission pile this time yielded up stories by writers like Ronan Doyle, Antonia Hart, Róisín McDermott, Kathleen Murray and John Saul, all of whom were completely new to me. If the mission statement reminds me what it is we're supposed to be doing, then stories like theirs serve to remind me why.

With twenty-two stories on board, I am not going to attempt to offer any sort of synopsis or analysis of individual stories. Nor am I going to expound upon common themes or preoccupations.

All stories have the ability to reflect the life as lived in a particular place and time, and the short story form is probably better equipped than the novel to keep pace with our rapidly changing world. Life as we know it in 2006—the outward signs—is certainly reflected in most of these stories, but they are about much more than that.

The power of the short story lies in its ability to take us beneath the surface of things. They make us believe that we are being granted full and immediate access into the heart of another person's life. The good writer will ensure that whatever may happen within the fictional world of the story, the reader will recognise it as being true.

The late, lamented John McGahern said of his motivations for writing that 'you write because you have to... We can say that writing memorialises, stops time, allows us to see more clearly, enables us to find out certain things; but eventually we write because we have to.'

For McGahern what mattered was not the material a writer had at his or her disposal, but how the writer elected to handle this material, what he or she made of it. 'Everything interesting begins with one person, in one place,' he said. He also believed that the two essential figures in literature are the writer and the reader. Everyone else involved, including publishers and editors, are just 'necessary paraphernalia'—necessary so that these two figures can be connected, so that books can find their readers.

With this in mind I think I've said more than enough, and it's time I stepped aside and allowed you a clear run at these stories. Enjoy.

Declan Meade
Publisher/Editor

Dublin, June 2006

These Are Our Lives

Party at Helen's

Kevin Barry

How does a boy born to a place of dismal fields and cold stone churches turn out to be fuck-off cool? How do you compute boreens and crows and dishwater skies and make it add up to a nineteen-year-old who walks into a party and every girl in the place goes loop-the-loop?

But not walks—walked. The party has been over for fifteen years. It was in Galway, on a Saturday night, after the nightclubs had closed and the late roar of the streets had started to break up. A couple of dozen people—you'd say children, if you could see them now—went back, in pairs and in small groups, to a rented house. Most of them were still pretty mashed on cheap nightclub drugs. The house had tongue-and-groove walls greening with damp and was filled with the smell of the damp and with the cloying waft of a low-grade cannabis resin. It was a little past four. The panes of the sash windows trembled with vibration from the music that was playing and the miserable furniture was pushed back to the walls. He went alone to a vantage corner. He hunched down on his heels and scoped out the ground. The girls wore lycra and had their hair styled in blunt retro fringes, like Jane Fonda in Barbarella. They wore clumpy shoes and tiny silver dresses, or flight jackets with heavy fur collars, they wore Lacoste, Fila and Le Coq Sportif. He sized them up, one by one, from ankles to nape, and he paid special attention to the tendons and the neck muscles, like a canny young farmer at mart.

He made his decision, quickly and without fuss. He crossed the room towards where she was dancing and he said hi. She ignored him. He felt dry-mouthed, tense with concentration, excited. He would need to follow her eyes, carefully, and find the words that might lighten them. This was work. She was aloof and this had its magneticism and he may have begun to despair but he received a quick enquiring glance from over her shoulder and so was heartened. Gesture politics, in an old house, on a rough winter's night, down a backstreet of Galway. There was water moving nearby, it wasn't far from the Claddagh. She had a hindquarter on her it was unbelievable.

'I saw you at Wiped, yeah?'

'Yeah?'

'Yeah. What was your name again?'

'Martina.'

Two words were enough to give it away as a Clare accent, flat and somehow accusatory, an accent he didn't like, normally, but she was good-looking enough to get away with it. His accent was from further north, and a shade west, it was pure Roscommon. It was designed for roaring over chainsaws and slurring ballads to the fallen martyrs of Irish republicanism but he had honed it, somehow, to a hoarse-sounding, late-night cool.

Around them, all was nervousness and elation. Lit up like stars, everybody loved everybody, and there was little shyness about saying so. Hugs and love and tearful embraces. It was all tremendously fluffy. These were children born to unions of a pragmatism so dry it chaffed, they came from supper tables livid with silence, they came down from marriages where the L-word hadn't darkened the door in decades. There was the feeling of sweat from the nightclub cooling on the small of your back.

He wore a number two cut, it was Daxed and brushed forward, and the sideburns were daily tended to. He by habit checked out people's shoes: she was wearing Fila creepers, of which he approved. He owned 387 12-inch records, mostly from Berlin, Sheffield or Detroit. He had a father with a head like a boiled ham.

'It's coming on in waves, like.'

'Yeah,' she said, 'I know what you mean.'

Not by any stretch of the imagination could you say she had big tits but fine, really, at least not like your one out of the art college the other week, like an ironing board she was.

'Waves,' he said, and he chewed his jaws, and he rolled his cowtown shoulders.

The windows shuddered with bass and rattled with wind. There were the usual January gales off the Bay. It was one of those nights you'd be skinned walking down Spanish Arch, if you were heading for the taxis on Dominick Street. He weighed up his chances of getting her into a taxi and out the far end of Salthill. He lived in a bedsit there the size of a shoebox. He could make tea and toast without getting up out of the bed. It was a row of old seaside boarding houses, mostly in disrepair. He could see down to the prom, to the low breaking waters and the power walkers in vivid rain gear, such garish colours in the rain. He sometimes followed random women on the prom. Yummy-mummies, coming out of mass or the Centra: he walked at a reasonable distance behind, and was pleasantly hypnotised by the swaying quick switches of their rears. He almost always managed to control himself but sometimes they were very pale and beautiful. He scribbled down their car regs, just to mark the sighting, for no other purpose than that. He kept a list of regs and descriptions in a folder beneath his bed.

Only once had he become fevered. That was the day he followed the woman to her house on Taylor's Hill. He had hauled up over the high wall and huddled in the wet garden behind her hedge. He peered into the kitchen—the light was on at three o'clock, it was such a dark afternoon—and he watched her boil a kettle for tea, the steam rising out of it, and the blood rushing in his ears. This was the most erotically-charged moment of October. He was on ketamine at the time.

'Waves, like,' he said. 'You know? I think I'm coming up on the third one now. I wouldn't be surprised.'

She sensed something about him. When he looked at you, handsome and sharp-featured though he was, you got the feeling that comes after you've chewed a mouthful and you just know that the chicken is dodgy. She moved away from him. She went to her friend, Alice. She asked Alice if she knew him.

'To see,' said Alice. 'Majorly cute. You must have seen him around the place. At Wiped and that. At Sex Kitchen?'

'Yeah but why is he always on his own though?'

'Maybe he's just a bit quiet,' said Alice.

Alice had a forgiving nature, especially when it came to men. She could find a good word to say about most anything in pants. She came from Tipperary and was the shape and texture of a kiwi fruit. She was so button-nosed you would think to press on it and hear a bell. She stood a jaunty five-nothing in her tallest heels. She was vivid, emotionally, and would make an opera out of the smallest crisis. She feared the routine and the humdrum. She sensed how easily these might overwhelm the paltry glamour available to a small wet college town in the west of Ireland. She was intuitive: she had an idea of the vast adult dullness that loomed around the next turn. She shook her head to be rid of the thought, for tonight she was hellbent on fun.

She drifted away from Martina, politely, still smiling. She loved her friend dearly but Martina was five ten and supple as a fawn: in the foreground perspective of a house party, the contrast-gain would not be Alice's. She went to the kitchen, where there was a congregation too sophisticated to dance, or too smashed, or too shy. Alice's gift was to immediately offer herself as an intimate and to be accepted as such. People let it all hang out when they talked to Alice. She enjoyed this but it could be a burden too. She was left with little space for her own worries. Even her father had spilled to her, always, even when she was a kid, shit she didn't need to hear. This had made her mother jealous, even though she couldn't understand why, and it helped to further corrode a failing marriage. Theirs was the first divorce in Tipp after divorce came in.

Alice in the kitchen sat by Mary Pearson, and took her by the arm, and they listened, with glazed smiles, as Obran rattled on and on at one of his endless, self-aggrandising yarns. Mary kissed Alice's button nose and laid her long, elegant fingers across Alice's nervous knees. The manner of this, the lanquid ease of it, edged just a shade beyond chumminess. Mary Pearson had deep sexual talent and was becoming ever more comfortable in its realm. She was a slender, fine-boned twenty, plain-featured but attractive, with that particular charge of attractiveness that comes in freckles and neat chin and dirty eyes, and she applied it through the touch of her fingertips and Alice moved on again, bashful now. The kitchen stank of Wednesday's bolognaise and of drying sweat.

Mary listened to Obran ramble on, bollocks talk, and she watched Alice join another small huddle, and she watched the stunned, wordless lads from Connemara who had eaten too much ecstasy, and she smiled for Jack and Kay. She watched over them all with the fondness that is usually reserved for watching over small children. She was born to middle age, and a lascivious one: all solace was in the senses. She'd slept already with three of the boys and two of the girls at the party. She'd been notching them off in History and Politics, and she was working her way through the hockey union too. Her father owned half Ballinasloe. She had not talked to him since the horse fair, when he'd accused her of sleeping with an itinerant. She bored of Obran—anyway she'd already been there—and she crossed the kitchen towards Jack and Kay, she was convinced she could talk them into it yet. Ollie stumbled as she passed and almost knocked her over.

'Ollie! For fucksake. Watch where you're going.'

'Lady Muck,' said Ollie, bowing. 'My most sincere apologies, like.'

Ollie moved on through the hallway. He paused to steady himself with a hand on the hall table. The hall table had flyers for pizza and Jesus. That snot-nosed bitch, the look she always gave him. He peeped into the main room and it was writhing now, there had been a fresh intake from a party in Salthill broken up by guards. He decided that he had no interest at all in the main room. His business was done for the evening and anyway he felt short-breathed and tense and his vision was definitely blurred, especially out of the left eye. He went upstairs instead. He wore his puffa jacket, as he did at all times. He stuck his beany, bristled head into a small boxroom, saw that it was empty, and gratefully threw himself down on its lonesome single bed. Ollie had overdone it, again. Ollie had been overdoing it, in one way or another, since he was big enough for shoes. His eyes were frightened and atrocious, pissholes in the snow, and they gave him a comically tormented look, always, even if he was in good form. He was local. He sold amphetamine cut with paracetamol to students, and he signed on at three post offices, one in the city and two in the county. He drove a Fiesta that was rotten with rust, it had neither tax nor insurance. He smoked too much cannabis. He drank like it was going out of style. He no longer had parents, he had six brothers who between them had six wives, nineteen children and twenty-eight dogs. His brothers would slag him about the seventh bride but Ollie had no interest in women, nor in men for that matter, he had interest in money, cannabis, cars, amphetamines and long-neck bottles of Corona lager. He had a kind of antic court jauntiness, almost medieval-seeming. There was no violence in him. There was vast bitterness in him. He made up stories out of the wet salty air, about people and for people, to frighten them and to entertain. He was currently putting it about that Mary Pearson had HIV. He was subject to magical thinking about the significance of the number nine. He put together a fat cone that used up five Rizlas and two entire Rothmans. He sucked down the lovely resins and immediately took on the notion that there were guards outside the house. They could have followed the crowd that came in from Salthill, you see. Of course they could have. It wasn't just likely it was probable. He took another drag and felt his crown tighten and he decided it was certain, he didn't have a minute to spare. He went to the window and looked down to the parked cars, and to the shadows, and the rain coming in slantwise and persistent. There were plainclothes out there, of course there were, and they were waiting for him to make his move. Well, they hadn't bested him yet and they wouldn't tonight. It was Ollie's belief that he was tailed by plainclothes five or six days out of the week and he wasn't entirely mistaken in this. The window was an attic window—a cheap velour job set into the slate roof—and he saw that if he took off the puffa it would be easy enough to wriggle outside, he was slim-hipped as a ferret, and he could move along the rooftops of the terrace that the house was set on. Puffa out the window, and he climbed after it, with the cone wedged efficiently in the corner of his mouth, glowing. From the rooftop you could see to the cathedral, its wet concrete looming through the foul weather, and distant, the blur of the taxi-lights in rain, and all around the sodium gloom of the lamps. Ollie zipped up into the puffa again and patted himself down to check for wallet and keys, lighter and fags and dope. He pressed back against the dripping slates and worked out his escape. He counted the chimneys along the length of the terrace—nine. He would need to climb to the other side, over the crease of the rooftop, and from there he could shin down a drainpipe into a yard, and then make his way down back towards the docks. So long as there were no dogs he'd be fine. He set to.

'Who'd leave a window open on a night like this? It's an icebox in here.'

'Actually the breeze is kind of nice now, leave it open a while. Whose room is it anyway?'

'Probably Shane's. It certainly smells like a wankpit.'

'Does, doesn't it?'

'Well, if it's Shane we're talking about, there'll be no shortage of action,' and he made the jerk-off motion with his hand.

'Please, Jack. Not an image I want to stick. He's not here, is he?'

'Think he's at home still. There are cows to be milked in Leitrim. There is no such thing as Christmas for cows, you know. Come here to me.'

'Fuck off.'

'What?'

'What what? Do you honestly believe I might be feeling romantic?'

'You're making too much out of this.'

'Easy for you to say.'

'Oh. I thought the plan was we weren't going to talk about it. Tuesday it's done with and we can forget about it.'

'It was crazy taking a pill.'

'What difference does it make, Kay? You're getting it looked after on Tuesday.'

'Looked after! This is starting to sound like something from the 1950s.'

'I know, yeah. She takes the lonesome boat. I am in the moody, guilt-ridden role. It's a play-of-the-week starring Cyril Cusack and Joan McKenna. Can you hear the uillean pipes?'

'Siobhan McKenna. Anyway nothing's decided.'

'Don't. Everything is decided. We've been all around the houses with this, it's set for Tuesday. We do it and it's done.'

'I'm the one up on the table!'

'Boo-hoo. So fine, okay. Tell you what. Let's have it then. We'll buy a semi-d and sign up for Fianna Fail.'

'You're an asshole. Why don't you go and rub off Mary Pearson some more?'

'Maybe I shall, maybe I shall,' and he made the cross-eyed look, and he did the Twilight Zone music, and she laughed.

'What are we going to do, Jack?'

'Another half?'

'Unbelievable! Really, I mean you're outdoing yourself tonight.'

'I know. I'm an absolute maggot. And you adore me, so deal with it. And come here, look? Please.'

She could taste a mercury note in her mouth and she wondered if this was in some way connected. She rose to leave. She was quickly getting towards the end of Jack. She saw that all was used to reinforce his masculine place in the world. All was weighed and tested for advantage. In everything that occured, he saw possibilities for developing his own sense of himself: he had used the crisis merely to give a burnish to his self-importance.

'Where you going?'

'Stay where you are, Jack, I'm just getting some water. I'll be a second.'

Everytime she left his presence she felt a delicious lightness come on her, a silk scarf placed on bare shoulders. She went lightly down the stairs and into the late throb of the party. The house was full of music and breathless talk and attempted romance but just as it peaked it began to fade, too, and people were tiring some, they were beginning to splay out on the cushions on the floor. The cheap drugs were wearing off and Sunday morning had begun to announce itself. It threw rain against the windows, like handfuls of gravel and nails, and there was stomach cramp and dryness of the mouth and morbid thoughts. Kay went to find her coat. The coats were in a pile behind the record decks and she winked at the dour-faced Northerner playing records.

'Kay, what about you?' he said.

'Alright, Chris?'

His world was round, twelve inches in circumference, and made out of black vinyl. He had tight hair composed of tiny curls and he would take a curl and twiggle it between thumb and forefinger, a nervous tic. His calling was to educate the west of Ireland to the pleasures of old-skool Detroit techno. The trouble with this town was that people didn't want to know. They wanted to listen to the same old same old, week in week out. They wanted the big tunes. They wanted the cheesy stuff. Well, they could look elsewhere. He wasn't going to play ball. If they didn't like it, they could piss off. If they wanted cheese, they could go down and listen to Sonny Byrne. They'd deserve each other, Sonny Byrne and that crowd. Fucking mouth-breathers the pack of them.

'Do you know what I'm saying, Kay?'

But she was gone, she'd headed for the door, in a swish of auburn hair and a fun-fur coat. Little Miss Thing. Not that the thought hadn't crossed his mind. What she was doing with the other creature he would never know. Jack Keohane? An excuse for humanity. An egomaniac. But that was this town all over, wasn't it? It was all surface. Sometimes he wondered why he troubled himself with these people at all. They hadn't a notion. To prove the point, he put on an old Derrick May, one of the first Rhythm Is Rhythm things—genius!—and he surveyed the room owlishly as it kicked in but no. They just didn't get it. He twiggled a tiny curl between thumb and forefinger. He chewed a lip and sulked. He had enough of the place. He was going to take off, no question, one of these fine days, they wouldn't see his arse for dust. They'd be sorry then, and they listening to Sonny Byrne and his cheese—big fucking piano tunes. The major problem would be the shipment of the records. There were several thousand and that amounted to serious dead weight. Everybody was sprawled and splayed, they were lying wrapped around each other on the floor. A handful of gravel against the window. He'd just put on an Orb album and leave it at that. It was as much as they deserved. He went through to the kitchen to search out Noreen. There was no sign of Noreen.

'Nice set, Chris,' said Helen.

'Oh was it,' he said, 'was it really now? So what the fuck are you doing in here?'

She huffed out of the kitchen. The sooner somebody took that arsehole to one side and sorted him out, the better. Helen Coyle, if she insisted on anything, insisted that life should be mannerly. She was a petite dark-haired girl, carefully arranged, with an expression of tremendous pleasantness and openness. She thrived on neatness in all things. She had been at a loss, tonight, when she realised that her affairs had spun out of control. She was in the process of leaving Eoin for James. She sat on the stairs and reviewed the situation. She had not quite informed either of her plans. She felt that she had put enough out in the way of suggestion and signals, that they should each be able to grasp the new reality.

Dealing with men was like dealing with infants. If they weren't puppy-dog, they were crude and arrogant, and which was worse? She wasn't ever taking ecstacy again. It brought all this emotional crap up. And it… just… wasn't… neat. She put her head against the bannister and closed her eyes. Eoin, in her opinion, had already stalled in life. When they first went out, he'd seemed to have everything opening up for him. He was rangy, good-looking, quick-witted, he was fit and active, he didn't drink much or smoke much or do drugs much, he was sociable and presentable. But slowly, in the two years of their relationship, his terrible secret had slipped out: he was a settler. He would settle for the small solicitors firm in Galway. He would settle for a quiet, unperturbed life. He would settle for a house on Taylor's Hill and a new Saab on a biannual basis, and he would involve himself delicately in the probate of small farmers and shopkeepers, and he would father unassuming and well-spoken children. But not with Helen Coyle he wouldn't.

James, who was, inevitably, Eoin's best friend, had a wider reach to his ambition. He was a broad-beamed, meat-faced man—at just 22, there was none of the boy left—and he moved across the ground with a sure-footedness born of privilege. He had subtly courted Helen Coyle for the two years she had been involved with his friend—in the end, not all that subtly—because he had recognised early that in back of the pleasantness and openness there was an overwhelming want for progress. He saw that they would propel each other forward, through all the years and the bunfights, that neither would allow the other to slacken, not for a moment. James was handsome but in the way that a bulldog is handsome and in the cause of advancement he would have the grip and clench of a bulldog's jaws. That was good enough for Helen Coyle— she'd made her decision.

Slowly, with a sense of building unease, the night gave away on itself. The slow fog of the mood drugs lifted and left nothing at all behind. Still there was some low music and people lay on the cushions and couches, and Alice, button-nosed, slept on her arms at the kitchen table. There was a tiny snoring sound if you crept up and listened to her quietly, and she dreamt of faraway places and pleasant young men in a warm light.

The nineteen-year-old from Roscommon had been rebuffed at every turn and he prepared for a cold wet walk out the long curve of the bay to Salthill. He would not spend on a taxi if there wasn't cause to. They would already be unwrapping bundles of newspapers outside the churches and the gulls, raucous with winter, would circle down from the low sky in search of last night's chips.

Helen went to her room upstairs and she quickly, neatly undressed and she stood for a moment with her left hand laid on her flawless belly, the satisfaction of that, and her pert nose twitched, she believed that she could smell smoke. She put on her dressing gown and followed the smell, it came from down the hallway, from the boxroom. She pushed in the door and saw Jack asleep on the narrow bed and the filthy old carpet smouldering on the floor. It was clear at a glance what had happened. His cigarette had fallen but there had been a piece of luck, he had the window open and rain had come in and put out the few flames that had started. It was almost at the finish of its damp smouldering by now. She went to find Chris, who shared the house, and a bucket of water, just to be sure. Fucking Jack. He could have put the whole place up, these houses were always going up, every year the *Advertiser* had another dreary tragedy, with names and ages and places of origin, from Carlow, originally, from Roscommon, originally.

Chris was back in the living room, flicking through his records. She whispered it to him. Fucksake! he said. Fucking typical of these people! There's another deposit gone! He ran upstairs and saw that it was as she said—he didn't and he never would trust women's accounts of things—and he went to fetch the water. When she had bent down to whisper to him, he turned just in time to see the swell of a breast beneath the dressing gown and the image now occupied his mind to a far greater degree than the non-event of a failed fire.

Martina turned to Mary Pearson, on a couch pushed back to the living room wall, and she said:

'Dave Costelloe? Yeah, but… kind of low-sized, isn't he?'

'I know. It's the kind of way that if he was three inches taller he'd be a different man.'

'Yeah but I do know what you mean, he's kind of dirty?'

'Oh, filthy! There is absolute filth in those eyes.'

'Yeah, there is but… Jesus. Can you believe the time?'

'Great. Sunday's a write-off. Come here, do you want to go and get some breakfast? I'm pretty sure Anton's is open.'

It was eight o'clock, in Galway, on a Sunday morning. The wind had eased, to some extent. It would be a cold day with intermittent rain. Ollie drove the Fiesta down the docks, his beany head swivelling left and right. He had people to see at the Harbour Bar, which kept market hours, and he had only the one wiper working. In rain, it felt as though the Fiesta was gone half-blind. His shin was reefed open from the drainpipe but the wound had dried up some and all told it was unlikely to kill him. He passed by the house and wondered if there was anything still going on in there. If things worked out at the Harbour Bar, he could knock back up and do some more business. But just as he drove past, the last of the stragglers emerged to the grey old streets and to another wet morning of the reconstruction.

Speechless

Antonia Hart

IAN PURSED HIS LIPS FOR A KISS, but didn't move, so Anna laid her napkin aside, pushed back her chair and leaned across the plates and glasses to reach him. She sat down.

'You have gravy on your skirt,' he said. 'You're like a child, so messy.'

Anna's cheekbones warmed. She looked at her plate and counted the flecks of scallion in her mashed potato. If she counted every piece he would apologise and move on to something else.

'I was joking,' he said. 'Don't take it so seriously, for God's sake.'

Anna counted the scallion bits which had only green, no white.

'Oh, Jesus.' Ian scrunched his napkin and flung it onto the table.

Anna kept her eyes down and built a wall of scallion bits across the front of her brain so that his remarks could not penetrate. He was shouting now. People at neighbouring tables glanced over their wineglass rims at them, then looked at each other.

'You are so unbelievably rude!' He slammed a hand flat on the table. 'Answer me when I'm speaking to you!'

Anna clutched at her bag, rose and knocked her chair away from under her with the backs of her knees. When he shouted and started flinging things around she had to get away at the first possible moment, because the noise would get into the weak bits of her brain and make them crumble. She left the restaurant and stumbled down the street, waving for a taxi. When she got in she leaned against the window, turned off her phone and savoured the taxi driver's simple questions.

'Yes, yes, thanks, that's right, just here.'

In bed, Anna pulled the duvet over her face and lay in her clothes until two or three in the morning. She woke from a doze, starving, desperate to eat. She threw two eggs into a pan of water, and as soon as the water started boiling, she grabbed the eggs and spooned out their messy insides. The whites had only just started to turn opaque and solidify against the shells, and she slurped them with the yolks. She drank two cans of beer straight off, then half a litre of milk.

When she woke the next day with a metal taste in her mouth and stains on her pyjamas she remembered that she'd thrown up the eggs and milk and beer. She showered with the water turned up to its hottest, and shampooed her hair three times, scrubbing and scraping with her nails on her scalp. She made up her face, thickly. *Eyes or lips,* the magazines always said, *pick one or the other to emphasise.* She went dramatic on the eyes, sweeping dark shadow over her upper lid, flicking up at the corners and coating her lashes three times with mascara. She wasn't convinced of the effect but she didn't look as if she'd spent the night crying and puking raw eggs, and so would face no questioning when she went to work at the shop. She rubbed foundation the colour of skin into her lips until the skin started to flake away.

The shop was not busy that day, but she decided to stay at the counter over lunch instead of putting up a closed sign. She thought Ian might phone. It would be better to be talking to him in the quiet shop than in a café with people listening and the noise of their chatter drowning his voice so she would have to say What? What? and it would stoke his rage and he would hang up.

She bought a smoothie for her lunch and sucked it up slowly through a straw. He didn't phone, so she did, on the shop phone, which she wasn't supposed to do, and said she was sorry.

'What are you sorry for?' He didn't mean, you have no reason to be sorry. He meant, spell out the reasons you have to be sorry.

She sighed. The corners of her mouth prickled.

'I'm sorry for last night.'

The little bell over the door jingled, and a woman came into the shop.

'What about last night?' he persisted.

She chewed her lip, tasting foundation. The customer made eyebrow signals at her, waving the fountain pen she'd chosen.

'Could you hold on a minute?' she muttered into the phone, and turned to box and wrap the pen and swipe the credit card. When she picked up the phone again he had gone.

She took the bus home, leaning uncomfortably against a pole. As the bus swung and jolted round corners her bag slipped off her shoulder and lodged in the angle made where her hand stuck into her pocket. Her insides were tight and full. A girl of about seven on the seat opposite stared at her, then slid from her seat to get a closer look.

'Are you having a baby?' she asked.

Anna swallowed with difficulty and looked to the girl's mother, who was sending text messages and did not reproach her daughter.

'Because your tummy is really fat,' said the girl, 'and when your tummy gets fat a baby comes out.'

Anna looked at her and thought of the things she could say—the hurt things, the rude things, the educating things, the squashing things—and then she let her eyes glaze over, slowly, so that the little girl wouldn't be sure they hadn't always looked like that. She acted as if she hadn't heard, and as if the little girl were invisible. If I do have a baby, she thought, please let it never grow up to be seven and and stare at people's stomachs, which are no fatter than they should be, and make people need to cry on buses. Your body should act in your interest. It should be protected from other people, and it should protect you. People should not be able to do things to it, to make it act differently, to put its actions beyond your control. It should retain its shape, not ask for more food than it needed, not ask for food only to reject it. It should lead you to sleep only with men who wouldn't betray you. It should conceive a child when a child was wanted and needed, and it should conceive a child only if it were in a position to support it for nine months. It should not disclose its internal events by external signs. Bloodstains on the seat of your jeans, swollen premenstrual breasts, the monthly layer of oil on skin and hair—all of these meant you had no privacy. Your body simply was not something you could either rely on or control, but you had to try.

At home she washed the drama off her eyes and gave them a good scrubbing with a corner of towel. She found she couldn't open her mouth properly to brush her teeth, so she slotted the brush in carefully, avoiding the corners of her mouth, which stung and needed to be kept closed.

Ian didn't call, so she rang him.

'Sorry about lunchtime,' she said.

Speaking was getting uncomfortable. The corners of her mouth were scabbing over.

'Why ring me if you're going to leave me hanging on for ten minutes?' he demanded.

Anna said nothing.

'Well?' He would be getting going again any minute.

To apologise, Anna thought, I rang you to apologise, and to give you the opportunity of apologising without having to be the one to ring, and I was worried because yesterday we were in love and then suddenly the last thing possible was to share anything with you. I rang you to get back to being in love with you but you hung up on me.

She rubbed her cuff over the telephone keypad, brushing away dust. She said nothing.

'Are you there?' Ian sounded tired now.

'Mmm,' said Anna.

'Well, what do you want me to do?'

'Come over?' asked Anna.

It would be easier face to face, with expressions and hand gestures to help, and she might find herself able to explain to him what was happening inside her.

He came over and said it was all right and he was sorry he'd lost his temper, but really she was so infuriating, and Anna nodded and muttered that she knew she was, and she came to sit beside him on the sofa and he sort of slapped her thigh in a friendly way to indicate that the argument was over. Then he peered a little more closely at her face.

'Do you have a cold sore?'

She touched along her lips. 'No.'

He looked closer.

'You do. Two of them, actually. Two massive ones, one each side.

You'd want to put something on those. Don't mind if I don't kiss you, do you?'

She did not mind if he never kissed her again. She didn't want his lips wetting her face, the smell of his saliva as it dried on her lips, his chin knocking against hers, his nose jamming into her eye. Kissing was the last thing she wanted.

'I'm tired,' she said. 'I didn't sleep well last night.' She suppressed a yawn in a way that she knew annoyed him, with her mouth pulled long but kept closed, and her nostrils inflating to pull in the extra oxygen. He looked away, and she stood up, and the evening was over.

In the shop the next day, Anna spoke as little as possible, because her mouth was getting sorer and the scabs at the corners were growing towards one another. She served customers with smiles and gestures, and no one seemed to notice anything, which was perfect, because she knew that soon she wouldn't be able to speak even if she wanted to, and she needed to practise silent communication while she could still speak in emergencies.

Ian thought they were cold sores, and it suited him to think that, but she knew he was wrong and that her mouth was shrinking and shrinking down to a tiny hole between her nose and chin, and that one day it would close completely.

A Very Unsettled Summer

Philip Ó Ceallaigh

It WAS A VERY UNSETTLED SUMMER. The hot weather had come and you tried in the day to walk in the shade and some nights only a sheet covered you as you slept. But there were also far too many days of atmospheric disturbance—electricity in the sky and a strange metallic taste in the mouth—when it was oppressively humid and heavy clouds massed very slowly through the long afternoons. People complained of headaches. And as the night came the clouds made final sense and broke, and you felt you had been holding your breath all day and could breathe again, and you went out onto your balcony, if you had a view, and looked across the city at the spectacle of inundation, and you nearly wanted to laugh at the cat scuttling across the road, caught in the white lightning flash, the city lit up and trembling with thunder and wetness, the horizon crackling with electricity. It was quite beautiful.

Unfortunately, coming home one of those humid afternoons, his clothes a damp weight, wishing it would happen, whatever it was, he found a bulky brown envelope in the postbox. His name and address were written in ink, by hand. He got in the lift and opened the envelope and on the first of several typed pages was written, in very large letters:

HOW I BECAME A WHORE

He read the first few lines. It was a story, it seemed. He looked at the envelope again and recognised the handwriting. They had been together for several years and had split up the previous summer. The end of it had come, to his surprise, as a relief. So now she was writing stories. Well, many people did. And poems. To get their feelings down. He smiled. He did not expect much of the story. But at least it was short, and she had chosen a good title. There was no accompanying letter. Not even a note. The lift stopped. He stuffed the pages back into their envelope. He entered the apartment, put the car keys and the envelope on the hall table, took off his tie, went to the bathroom and urinated. He splashed cold water on his face, took off his shoes and left them in the hall. He stripped and took a quick cool shower. He put on shorts and a T-shirt and padded barefoot to the kitchen and took a beer from the fridge. He uncapped it and immediately drank a third of the contents. Then he picked up the envelope, which he had not forgotten while he was freshening up, and took it to the living room.

He arranged the cushions on the sofa, put his feet up, took a pull of beer and read the story.

It went like this:

It described, from the perspective of his ex-girlfriend, one of the several times they had split up and him saying a number of banal things over a bottle of wine in a bar. The girl in the story hides her feelings of anger and humiliation and does some quick thinking. She offers the man sex for money. She plays the whore. The narrator is at this point no longer his ex-girlfriend, strictly speaking. She has become a character in a story, as these things happen in dreams, where forms and identities are shifting and provisional. And, of course, he is no longer entirely himself either.

The female character has decided to gratify a fantasy the man has long had. Or is pretending to do so. This is not entirely clear. In any case, the man takes the bait. They play the game. He has to show her the money in his wallet. They do the dialogue. He accompanies her to her place and admires it, saying business must not be bad.

He was reading eagerly towards the end, anticipating the sex scene, when things got slightly complicated.

They are in her kitchen ('with all the knives') and she has offered him something to drink, and he is drinking the red wine, smoking, and engaging in the foreplay of pre-sex talk and the narrator—her—says:

*I once prepared a rabbit. I marinated it well in red wine and herbs,
then cooked it slowly.*

*I looked at him and offered him another glass. He nodded readily
and I poured. He was excited and edgy. Like a rabbit scared of being
caught. On the wrong foot. He was all shiny eyed, looking forward
to fun.*

It's coming, bunny. The fun is coming.

The story ended there. He did not know what was supposed to happen
next. He was unsure what kind of a game was being played.

He masturbated quickly. Afterwards, cleaning up, he was a little
surprised at having reacted in such a way to words on a page. He
resumed his seat and continued drinking the beer and wondered was it
the strange weather that made him want to play a hard game of tennis,
or break something. He went and got another beer and sat drinking that,
still thinking about what he had read. It seemed a good story. Or
possibly it was simply that in reading it he had imagined himself in it,
and that was what made it good.

The ending was clever, certainly, the conflation of a sexual fantasy
and a dance of revenge. He did not recall ever having any interest in the
prostitute thing, but imagining playing the game with her, the author,
had excited him. Pure sex. None of the personal and situational
complications that compromised desire. And perhaps this was her way
of extending an invitation. Perhaps they would go on to meet weekly,
playing the sex game. He checked inside the envelope, thinking he
might have missed the note. No, there was no message. He looked out
his window, which had a view, and the world looked interesting. The
clouds suggested they were not prepared to procrastinate much longer.
But they had been saying that for a very long time.

He considered phoning her, but suspected he was being toyed with,
like the character in the story.

The humid air was congealing into high solid banks of raincloud.

He swigged the beer down and burped gently. His present girlfriend
was coming over later and he did not want her to see the story. He arose
and slid the pages under a pile of old magazines and decided he would

get rid of it shortly. It would be wiser to forget it.

In the dream he sees her naked. He is unable to move, unable to reach out. She holds herself proudly, her physical beauty heightened because it is now hers to deny or bestow. Her skin glows. A proud strange smile as she turns and walks from the room leaves him lying on the bed, not knowing if she will return. He does not know if the smile means that he is being mocked or promised his reward.

He awoke next to the naked sleeping body of his girlfriend. It was very early morning and there was little light. The long slim body beside him was very beautiful, yet it was not the body he needed.

This is very awkward, he thought, lying on his back, aroused, beside a gently sleeping girl, as the morning light began to grow in the room.

He was in the bar where they had first met. It was the day after the dream and he felt that he would meet her. He was not one for presentiments, because that meant feeling something would happen when there is no way to explain the feeling. Like believing in dreams, or horoscopes. But he was looking at the door when she walked through, and he was not surprised, and the division between dreams and waking reality was disturbed.

He tried to continue the conversation he had been having when she walked in but was distracted by her presence. Perhaps she was pretending not to have noticed him. He felt invisible, like a ghost, observing the scene.

He watched her speaking to men and wondered if she was sleeping with any of them.

The hoofed beast of jealous panic rode through him. It told him to physically interpose himself. It told him to get off the ground and fight. It's because I'm drunk, and I had that dream, he told himself, that I am thinking like this. I should go home and sleep.

But he stayed and drank more and late at night they were sitting at a table together. It was civilised and they spoke of people they both knew and matters unrelated to her fictional life as a whore, and when finally they got on to the story they discussed it rationally, as a piece of workmanship. Workwomanship. He told her he thought it was effective, and she smiled the smile he had seen in the dream.

Speaking to her, in real life and not in dreams or stories, steadied him and he found he was able to leave. Probably I took it all wrong, he thought, walking home. He was not interested in being wrong-footed. She was more attractive than he had remembered. Everything about her gave him an intense appetite.

Unfortunately, he thought, that is how it goes. Relationships entailing obligation entirely kill the flavour of erotic sport. It is never so attractive when yours for the taking.

In the end it did not involve laying down money, as in the story. It happened as these things do, talking and drinking, and moving on to bed.

He had spoken to her on the phone and then in the taxi to her place he felt sharp and high and energetic like on the crest of good drugs, the anticipation that the good news was about to be made flesh.

In the morning, he felt he had got her out of his system.

The second time that this sequence of events occurred he was also sure that he had resolved something. Walking home after the third time, he admitted to himself that it was not so simple.

Sometimes she would send him home unsatisfied. And that particular evening, with the electric storm moving in from the west, looked set to end that way. He had mentioned something about his girlfriend and she appeared unimpressed by the disclosure.

But he was drunk on her good red wine and began to tell her what had happened to him. 'It's not normal. It's like I have this intense physical pressure in my balls all the time, like when you are afraid or get an adrenalin rush and your scrotum tightens, like amphetamines kicking in, except it's all the time practically, and all I can think about is your body, the next time we'll meet, what way I'll give it to you. Like this massive pressure that just has to burst out.'

'Do you know,' she asked, 'Aristotle's definition of pleasure?'

He shook his head.

'Aristotle defined pleasure as the release from pain.'

She smiled, sweetly, he thought, and she tapped her cigarette in the ashtray. They were sitting on either side of a table.

'Let me suck it out of you. I'll drink it down and you'll feel better.'

He groaned quietly and slid down in his chair. She arose, walked over to him, kneeled down and opened his trousers. She rubbed her face against his thumping erection and smiled at him and continued looking into his eyes for the duration of some playful licking, then took it in her mouth, unhurriedly, as if she had never had anything so tasty in her life, and sucked him off and, as she had indicated, drank it all down. Then she got back on her feet, wiped her mouth with the back of her hand, drank a little water and lit a fresh cigarette. She returned to her place at the other side of the table.

He slouched, undone, like she had sucked the marrow from his backbone. He lit a cigarette too, with trembling hands. A delicious, dizzy cigarette.

'Feel better?' she asked with that smile he was coming to know. He was starting to understand that smile. It was a smile of control. A controlled smile.

'I'm not sure. I think so.'

He thought of a rabbit, marinated in red wine.

'So what's it like?' she asked. 'Having fun with someone who's not your girlfriend?'

The question was barbed, it seemed.

'Less domestic.'

Good reply. He wasn't losing his mind entirely. He inhaled the narcotic smoke deeply. The funny smile on her lips did not involve humour, however.

'Better, you mean? More exciting?'

He nodded, exhaled. Now he felt the less said the better. Anything could and would be used against him. Talk about the weather.

'Did you ever cheat on me, when I was your girlfriend?'

Now it was a scary smile.

'Come on. History.'

'Well, *did* you?' she pressed.

'Did *you*?'

Attack, the best defence.

'I asked first.'

The fact that she had not said no tripped his curiosity. He found the thought that she had been unfaithful without him guessing vaguely painful, and also pleasant, as the deepening of addiction always is. After all, it was not impossible. She had been jealous, clinging, moralistic and endlessly demanding. She had shown all the signs of obsession and wounded pride. But this did not mean there was never a moment, when she was annoyed with him perhaps, when something could have happened.

'Alright,' he said. 'I was not faithful.'

'How many times?'

Not enough fingers. Or toes.

'I answered. Your turn. Did you cheat on me?'

She nodded. 'I felt really bad about it.'

There was a lamp on the table. For a moment he thought it had begun to shake slightly. A minor seismic event, four or five on the Richter, could produce such jiggles. But it was his heart. His head was rocking to the beat of his heart.

The details came a bit too fast for him to take in. There were extenuating circumstances. She was feeling this, she was feeling that. They had had a fight one time. Another time he was away hiking in the mountains, being the man of nature, and she felt abandoned. With that one she'd never meant it to go on. But with the other it was just the once, they hadn't even talked on the phone afterwards, really just a quick thing, you know, over and done with. And that other time she was drunk, the time her handbag had got stolen and she had no keys, and she went to his place, not planning to do anything and, well, if he hadn't kissed her it would have been fine but you know how one thing leads to another. Then there was her ex. Well that didn't really count, she didn't feel like she'd cheated on him there; it was complicated, they had their own unresolved emotional business, nothing to do with him.

'But I felt kind of bad about that too.'

While he sat listening to her, with the storm moving in from the west, he just smoked and nodded, like he understood perfectly. Didn't do to look like you were being gutted. And, after all, it was all in the past.

Bollocks! Nothing was ever in the past. The past was a series of compartments which could unlock themselves at the least convenient moments.

He inquired about several details, then she yawned and said.

'History. Anyway, I have to get up early.'

'Can't I stay?'

Something in his voice that should not have been there had said, Can't I suck your titty, like a good baby?

She smiled a professional smile. 'Not tonight.'

The sky broke when he reached the street and he stood in the shelter of the doorway of her apartment building. Mentioning the girlfriend had been a big mistake. He considered going back up to borrow an umbrella. A taxi swished past in the rain, slowly, waiting for him to hail it, but he did not. An umbrella would be a good idea. But if he went back up there he would beg to be allowed stay. Fine, he was going to beg. Then he remembered how unpleasant it was when women behaved that way with him and he set off quickly through the downpour. For a moment he saw himself from afar, cinematically, punished by the heavy rain, walking down the boulevard of broken dreams. Then he was just a wet man in bad weather, and he was glad when the next taxi stopped.

In the days and weeks that followed he tried to construct, from what he remembered of her words, a plausible mental catalogue of her infidelities. It was an act of composition, a creative attempt to construct a complete picture, to use the imagination to bring memory and reality into some kind of accord. He recalled the visible part of their relationship—what they had been doing, how they had been acting at the time—and spliced in these new characters that had poked their way into their story. Poked their way! It was not funny. It was very painful. In this impossibly complicated saga he ruthlessly reduced himself to one more character, turning up in the intervals between her other erotic episodes.

Since putting such a project down on paper would be conclusive evidence of obsession, he tried to keep the calendar in his head, and was therefore always struggling to get purchase on his material.

But he could not stop himself, because the feeling that he had lived disconnected from reality terrified him. His memory, he now realised, had been fiction! He was trying to get a grip.

He began, for the very first time, to understand her jealousy. It was not a measure of greater devotion. It was simply that she had a better imagination than him. She imagined him doing. He had failed to imagine.

So he drove himself wild, trying to imagine his way back to reality.

It was during this period, when he had reduced himself to a character, that they played out most of his fantasies. These were for the most part variations on conventional themes. But he also found a number of ways to get the hit that he had not previously imagined, and in addition she came up with a few of her own, which both excited and unnerved him, because he had been with her for a long time and had had no indication. It was a bit like watching your wife getting fucked by another man. The edge of pain was the edge of pleasure, because in such moments he was both himself *and* the other man.

This meant, however, that the jealousy never left him when he was not there. The only time his existence did not seem to be on shaky ground was when he was inside her. He kept having to return, to subdue the anxiety with his flesh, as if by having her beneath him he could fuck the wildness out of her. As if, by having her ride above him, and come again, that he could finally satisfy her. It went on like that through the summer. There were very hot days, and electric storms, and such insistent precipitation that rivers burst their banks and you could watch on television the houses of the country people being washed away in the floods. God had promised he would never drown the whole world again but there were no guarantees that you were not going to get it on an individual or municipal level.

One evening, lying in a sweet fog of alcohol and the nearness of her skin and smell, he noticed it dangling from a hook on her bedroom wall. He was surprised he had not previously paid closer attention. It was a very plain rag doll—too ugly to be a child's toy—sown together from coarse sackcloth. It had two distinguishing features. It had a couple of funny rabbit ears. And it had a little cock and balls. More attention had gone into the latter equipment than anything else. The penis was a little red stick, in the erect position. The balls, out of scale, but gathered in anticipation.

'What,' he asked, pointing, 'is that?'

'That's my Bunny!'

She said it like Bunny was a special friend of hers.

'You're a bit big for stuffed animals.'

'A Bunny isn't for a little girl. Every girl gets a Bunny when she gets hair on her cunt.'

Bunny, she explained, had been brought to her by a friend who had visited an island in Indonesia. As a joke. She could not remember the name of the island. There were a lot of islands in Indonesia and Indonesia was a lot of islands. The story was that the women of the tribe each had one of these rabbit-men, which they kept near their beds in order to keep their men in order. The genital equipment was to keep the male inexhaustibly virile, while the ears were to keep them docile and prevent straying. He asked her how the men kept the women under control and she said she did not think it was that kind of tribe. The men had everything they needed and the women resolved their differences in a sisterly fashion. He took a drink of red wine and lit one of her cigarettes.

She got out of bed and took Bunny off his hook and gave him a squeeze. He winced. That is, the man winced, the subject of the story, not the rag doll, obviously. The red wine was getting to his guts. She gave Bunny's little wooden pecker a kiss and put him back on his hook. She got back in bed.

'They don't stick needles in it or anything?' he asked.

She laughed and reached out and gathered his balls and gave them a little squeeze.

'Silly!'

*

A giant crow was settled on his chest, ripping his heart with its beak, and he sat bolt upright and the bird flew away and dissolved in the ceiling and he saw the doll on the nail. He got up and went to the bathroom, remembering that Christ's path to crucifixion was called his Passion. The word passion meant suffering. That which must be passed through. She was sleeping with just the hint of a snore, the moonlight hitting her from the side, through the open window. Something was wrong with his guts. He quietly pulled on his clothes and made it to the street. He walked for a little and in the coolness felt better, briefly. Far skies crackled and rumbled, the storm pressing in slowly from across the western plain beyond the city. A jet of puke exploded from him, neon-orange puke beneath a streetlight, as the turbulence shook the trees and the sheet of rain hit the street a distance away and accelerated towards him. In seconds he was drenched by warm rain. The world went liquid. The sky was liquid and his guts were liquid, sloshing forth as he walked. He barely bothered to lean over, for it was instantly washed from him. It kept on coming as he pressed homewards through the deserted streets. He could not count how many times he had spewed. He was weak and incredulous. He had not eaten or drunk this much in the past week. There were impossible waterfalls of puke. Either it was an effect of the rain or he was hallucinating. Finally, as he approached home, there was retching, groaning, heaving and what he supposed was bile. There was battery acid in his mouth and the sky was shaking and crackling as the centre of the storm came closer. Fireworks were going off by the time he put the key in the door to his building. Lower, a sharp pain pressed his bowels. He got inside and made it to the toilet. More explosions of fluid. He was just a bag of shit and puke, at the mercy of corporal spasms. He finally fell into bed, weak and fevered. He had very bad dreams involving giant rabbits and tiny men.

To help himself recover, he wrote a story. To be the author rather than a character. He had read something I had done called *Scenes from a Kazakh Knocking-Shop* and felt I would be a receptive reader, though he admitted he was disappointed with aspects of the result. The first pancake of the batch always sticks to the pan and has to be scraped off,

I told him, flicking through the pages. I read it through as we drank vodka and grapefruit juice with big clanking ice cubes, sitting in my kitchen on a hot clear afternoon towards the end of summer, and when I had finished I told him I thought I could use it, if he didn't mind. He told me to go ahead. I got up and fixed us another couple of drinks.

'You know,' I said, 'it reminds me of how Nabokov got the idea for *Lolita*. He heard about this monkey, or ape, in the zoo in Paris. I suppose it was Paris. They gave it a sheet of paper and a crayon, to see what it would come up with. You know the very first thing it drew?'

He shook his head.

'It drew the bars of its cage.'

'Really?' he asked, sitting up straight and taking interest. 'You think this is in the tradition of Nabokov?'

'I was thinking more of the monkey.'

His life with his girlfriend, after his period of instability, or fuck-frenzy, whatever you want to call it, returned to normal. They had good times. They liked each other very much and they had interests in common. They went to the cinema together, took walks in the park, cooked new dishes, talked about books and films and made love unhurriedly. The lovemaking was just one more of those good things they did, and was a connected and natural part of those other things, and left him feeling clean and whole. And he was glad he had ridden out the madness and left it behind.

It is the nature of addiction that the craving lies dormant in every cell. Sometimes he would see a woman in the street and the old drug would buzz in his blood and his vision get muddy and mean. Then he would remember Bunny, hanging from his hook. Though it would be an exaggeration to say that this brought him to his proper senses, it did at least inhibit him.

The weather cleared. The electricity and precipitation moved on to torment another part of the planet, and the section he lived on enjoyed the clear sunny summer it had long hoped for. People had their picnics and barbecues, their trips to the beach, their mountain views.

Everything seemed to be going well. Unfortunately, when he was in his car one day, at a set of lights, on his way to take care of one of those trivial matters that must be attended to unless life in an urban metropolis is to unravel, his phone rang. It was his girlfriend. Choking with tears, she demanded to know the truth. Just the truth. She had found something he had written, read it, and reached a certain conclusion.

So that was the end of that story also, the walks in the park together, and all the rest of it.

Calais

John Saul

LATE AT NIGHT I CLAMBERED OVER THE FRONT SEAT and over Mona our driver sleeping and went for a walk. There was one last person on the square. He was cleaning up the hot dog papers and empty cans and pink and yellow lottery tickets which had scattered on the Calais road. He had a green cart and nylon brush and his name, he said, was Marek. He spoke a little French, a little German, a little English. We went to a dive he knew and drank a Stella Artois together. He told me he had left his wife and children in Gdansk. He didn't love his wife any longer, he did once of course. He was bored with her, she did not love him any more, and she did not like the way he spent so much time with his friend Pavel. She had been crying and sending letters and said he should come back and try all over again. But, he said, he saw no point in making a new start on what he knew would have the old end. He stood me another beer and I told him I was headed for fame as a film director. If he had a talent he could work for me. He could choose his profession and begin learning it now. He said he could imagine himself hairdressing, preparing the stars for the cameras. He could not be persuaded to raise his sights above that. Hairdressing—hair-cutting, he called it—was an honourable profession and had saved many injuries by preventing hair being caught in machines. I decided: he would be the first member of my crew. I stood him a beer and he told me that when he was a teenager he used to go to school with his hair bandaged in a turban so that he could grow it long the way people did in the West. Now that he was in the West himself, re-examining his life and turning all kinds of notions upside down, he had cut his own hair and enjoyed this so much he wanted to cut hair, not sweep streets. Suddenly a song on the jukebox upset him terribly and he went off to play a round of pinball. He came back and told me he had left his mother and father in Gdansk and this was his life's greatest dilemma. He did not want to abandon them and he did not want to stay in Gdansk. It was a dilemma he did not conceive of ever solving. Nonetheless he had to return to Poland. He was working entirely illegally and so far for only two days, or rather, nights. How, he asked, could he ever work for a film director in the West? Unless—he saw a way—I was prepared to film in Poland. But did Westerners really want to sit in cinemas and hear the various tragedies of Gdansk? Why not? I replied—it would be the new Poland, or the new Russia. My first masterpiece would begin with a bedroom scene, with Mona sitting on a bed in an autumn light, reading about the new Russia. Marek nodded. The jukebox had gone silent. He stood me one more beer and I felt cold and sick. I decided I would have to leave that very moment if I was to be able to clamber back into the car over the sleeping Mona, but I would keep my promise to Marek and so I gave him several phone numbers and addresses, ending in Nova Scotia. Nova Scotia was important because there I had an aunt who never moved. She was the fixed point in my universe, I told him, she had only to keep living and he would always be able to find me. Marek said he had an aunt in Potsdam and one day he would go there and visit the Sans Souci summer palace of Frederick the Great. Frederick the Great was a queer, he said. This was not widely known or mentioned but extremely obvious. He would see Sans Souci, which would always be like his Aunt Sophie remembered it. I felt bound to call this statement and asked him why. Because it was constantly renovated, he explained, a room at a time, round the palace and back to the beginning, in a never-ending cycle which lasted twenty years. The floors were kept smooth and shining by the visitors' pantoffles which, as mandatory footwear, polished them every day. The visitors laughed and grinned at each other, said his aunt, because they had to slide around like children on rinks of ice, and this is what the visitors best remembered. I told Marek that William Morris believed marble should be made to wear. Our conversation faltered at this point. I told him Cézanne the artist believed roads should not be straightened out with pavements. I told him John Fowles the novelist believed gardens should be left untended by human stewards. Live and let live, I said finally. He thought I was talking about a film involving James Bond. Marek stood up. He said he felt he had burst through the barrier of night exhaustion, and could go back and clean the square until it was very clean. He asked me for an English word meaning very clean and I said like a new pin. He said he would clean the square into a new pin. I expressed a wish to see this. Hands on his cart, we went back through the streets. On the way we met a sprinkler vehicle painted the same vivid green, edging tortoise-paced towards the square. He didn't clean at all after that, but mounted the cab of the sprinkler and waved goodbye. I clambered into the Fiat, collapsing so completely I was not certain I had not dreamed, inventing that just outside Calais I met a street cleaner whose name was Marek, and he came from Gdansk.

Dark Horses

Claire Keegan

IN THE NIGHT, BRADY DREAMS THE WOMAN back into his life again. She's out the yard with the big hunter, laughing, praising her dark horse. She reaches up, loosens the girth, and takes the saddle off. The hunter shakes himself, and snorts. At the trough she pumps fresh water. The handle shrieks when pressed but the hunter doesn't shy: he simply drops his head and drinks his fill. Further off, the cry of hounds moves across the fields. In his dream these hounds are Brady's own and he knows it will take a long time to gather them in and get them home.

Waking, he finds he's clothed from the waist down: black trousers and his working boots. He gropes for the clock, holds the glass close, reads the hands. It isn't late. Overhead, the light is still burning. He rises, pulls the string, and finds the rest of his clothes. Outside, the October rain goes shuddering through the bamboo. That was planted years ago to stake her shrubs and beans but when she left he took no mind, and the garden turned wild. On McQuaid's hill, through cloud, he makes out the figure of a man walking through fields greener than his own. McQuaid himself, herding, counting all the bullocks once again.

In the kitchen he boils water, scalds the pot. The tea makes him human again. He stands over the toaster and warms his hands. His Aunt Maggie brought up marmalade last week but there's hardly a lick in the jar. With a knife he scrapes what's left off the glass and goes out, in his jacket, to the fields. The two heifers need to be brought in and dosed. He must clear the drains, fell the ash in the lower field—and there's a good day's welding in the sheds before winter comes on strong.

He throws what's left of the sliced pan on the street and starts the van. A part of him is glad the day is wet.

In Belturbet, he buys drenching fluid, welding rods, oil for the saw. There's hardly any money left. He rings Leyden from the phone box, knowing he'll be home.

'Come up to the house,' Leyden says. 'I'm in need of a hand.'

It is a fine house on a hill which his wife, a schoolteacher, keeps immaculate. Two storeys painted white look out over the river. In the yard a pair of chestnut trees, the lorry, heads over every stable door. When Brady lands, Leyden waves from the hayshed. He's a tight man, bony, with great big hands.

'Ah, Brady! The man himself!'

'There's a bad day.'

''Tis raw,' Leyden agrees. 'Throw the halter on the mare there, would you? I've a feeling she'll give trouble.'

Brady holds the mare's head while Leyden shoes. The big hands are skilled: the hoof is measured, pared, the toe culled for the clip. On the anvil the shoe is held, hammered to size. Steel nails are driven home, and clenched. Then the rasp comes round and shavings fall like sawdust at their feet. All the while it's coming down, gasps of sudden rain whipping the galvanised roof. Brady feels strange pleasure standing there, sheltered, with the mare.

When Leyden rasps the last hoof, he throws the tools down and looks out at the rain.

'It's a day for the high stool,' he says.

'It's early,' Brady says uneasily.

'If we don't soon go, it's late it will be,' Leyden laughs.

'I've to get me finger out; there's jobs at home.' Brady puts the mare back in the stable, bolts the door.

'You'll come, any road,' Leyden says. 'I'll get Sean to change a cheque and we'll settle up.'

'It'll do another day.'

'Not a hate about it. I might not have it another day.'

'All right so.'

As Brady follows Leyden back to town, a burning in his stomach surges. Leyden turns down the slip road past the chemist and parks behind The Arms. It looks closed but Leyden pushes the back door open. The bulb is dark over the pool table. On *Northern Sound*, a woman is reading out the news. Long Kearns is there with his Powers, staring into the fishing net behind the bar. Norris and McPhillips are picking horses for the next race. Big Sean stands behind the counter, buttering bread.

'Is that bread fresh or is it yesterday's?' Leyden asks.

'Mother's Pride,' Sean smiles, looking up. 'Today's bread today.'

'But if we ate it tomorrow wouldn't it still be today's?' says Norris who has drunk two farms. Except for the slight shake in his hand, no one would ever know.

'Put up two of your finest there, Sean,' says Leyden, 'and pay no mind to that blackguard.'

'He's been minding me for years,' says Norris. 'He'll hardly stop now.'

Sean puts the lip of a pint glass to the tap. Leyden hands him the cheque and tells him to give Brady the change. The stout is left to settle, the dark falling slowly away from the cream.

'We got the mare shod, any road.'

'Did she stand?'

'It was terror,' Leyden says. 'I'd still be at it only for this man here.'

'It's a job for a younger man,' McPhillips says. 'I did it meself when I was a garsún.'

'After three pints there's nothing you've not done,' says Norris.

'And after two there's nothing you won't do!' says Leyden, raising the bar. 'Isn't that right, Sean?'

'Leave Sean out of it,' the barman says affectionately.

Norris looks at Brady. 'Is it my imagination or have you lost weight?'

Brady shakes his head but his hand reaches for his belt.

'It's put it on I have.'

Big Sean cuts sandwiches in half and leaves them on the counter. Brady reaches out but his hand closes on the glass. It seems to do so of its own accord. It isn't right to be drinking at this hour, and the stout is bitter.

'Have you a drop of blackcurrant there, Sean?'

'What are you doing with that poison?' Leyden asks. 'Destroying a good pint.'

'At least I didn't destroy four good hooves,' says Brady, finding his voice at last.

Everybody laughs.

'Is that so?' Leyden smiles 'And what would you know? There's nothing but cart horses in Monaghan.'

'Every cart horse needs shoes,' says Brady.

'They wear around the Cavan potholes,' says McPhillips, a Newbliss man.

'Now we have it!' Norris cries.

When the banter subsides, McPhillips goes out to place the bets. The silence is like the silence between waves; each man is glad of it and glad, too, that it won't last. Sean turns off the radio now that the news is over.

As they sit there in the silence, Leyden's nostril flares.

'Which one of ye dug up Elvis?'

'Lord God!' Long Kearns says, coming suddenly to life. 'That would knock a blackbird off its pad.'

Leyden swallows half his pint. The shoeing has put a thirst on him so Brady, not liking to leave with the money, orders another round.

Out in the street, school children are eating chips from brown paper bags. There's the smell of fried onions, hot oil and vinegar. It is darker now and the rain is still falling. When Brady walks into the diner the girl behind the counter looks up: 'Fresh cod and chips?'

Brady nods. 'Ay. And tea.'

He sits at the window and looks out at the day. Black clouds are sliding over the bungalows. He thinks again of that night in Cootehill. There was a Northern band in The White Horse. The woman could dance: all he had to do was lead her. They sat at the little table near the bandstand and talked about horses. Afterwards she asked him to come back to the house. *If you bring the chips, I'll light the fire and put the kettle on.* They ate in the firelight. A yellow cloth was spread over the table, her cutlery flashed silver. Smell of deodorant lingering in her bedroom, a wee candle burning, headlights passing through the curtains. When he woke, at dawn, she was asleep, her hand on his chest. He was working then, full time, for Leyden. That morning, walking down the main street of Cootehill, buying milk and rashers, he felt like a man.

The girl comes with his order. He eats what's placed before him, and pays. Out in the street, there are Christmas cards in the newsagents. Passing the hotel, he hears music. He goes in, sits at the counter, orders. A few songs are sung. The day is no longer his own. At some point he looks up and realises McQuaid is there, in a dark suit of clothes, with his wife. Sensing him, McQuaid looks over, nods. Soon after, a pint's sent down. On Brady's lips the stout is cold.

'The bowld man himself! Have you no home to go to?' It's Leyden. He takes one look at Brady, and changes. 'What's ailing you at all, man?'

Brady shakes his head.

Leyden looks over at McQuaid. The waitress is bringing serviettes, knives for the steak.

'Pay no mind,' he says. 'Not a hate about it. The land'll be here long after we're dead and gone. Haven't we only the lend of it?'

Brady nods and orders drink for Leyden.

'It's the woman that's your loss,' Leyden says unhelpfully. 'That was the finest woman ever came around these parts.'

'Ay,' Brady says.

'There's men'd give their right arms to have a woman like that.' Leyden says, coming in tight and taking hold of his right arm.

'They would, surely.'

'What happened at all?'

Brady feels rooted to the stool. Back then some days were hard but not one of them was wasted. He looks away. The silence rises.

'It was over the horse,' he says finally.

'The horse?'

Brady clears his throat. 'I came home one night and she told me I'd have to buy food, pay bills.'

'And what did you say?'

'I told her to go fuck herself!' Brady says. 'I told her I'd put her horses out on the road.'

'That's terror,' Leyden says. 'Did you have drink on you?'

Brady hesitates. 'A wee drop.'

'Sure we all *say* things.'

'I went out and opened the gate and let the horses out on the road,' Brady says. 'She gave me a second chance but it was never the same. Nothing was ever the same.'

'Christ,' says Leyden, pulling away. 'I didn't think you had it in you.'

It is well past closing time when Brady finds the van. He gets behind the wheel and takes the back roads home. It will be all right; the sergeant knows him, he knows the sergeant. He will not be stopped. There are big, wet trees at either side of these roads, telephone poles, wires dangling. He drives on through falling leaves, keeping to his own side. When he reaches the front door, the bread is still on the step. The dog hasn't come home but the birds will have it gone by morning. He looks at the kitchen table, climbs the stairs.

He gets into the wisp and takes his jumper off. He wants to take his boots off but he is afraid. If he takes his boots off he knows he will never get them on in the morning. He crouches under the bedclothes and looks at the bare window. It is winter now. What is it doing out there? The wind is piping terrible notes in the garden and, somewhere, a beast is roaring. He hopes it is McQuaid's. He lies in his bed thinking only of her. He can feel his own heart, beating. He closes his eyes. Soon, she will come back and forgive him. The bridle will be back on the coat stand, the cloth on the table. In his mind there is the flash of silver. As sleep is claiming him, she is already there, her pale hand on his chest and her dark horse is back grazing his fields.

Desire

Róisín McDermott

NOBODY REALLY KNOWS WHAT HAPPENED TO DELILAH'S HAIR. Of course the campus was abuzz with rumours all that spring and the gossip was first-class, high-octane stuff; but Delilah wasn't talking, and, needless to say, neither were the O'Haras.

The name Delilah entered Joyce's consciousness for the first time one chilly morning early in the winter term when she overheard two male students gossiping in the college library: 'Have you seen that American babe called Delilah in first year English?' whispered one. 'God yes— wouldn't mind being subdued by that!' breathed the other, as a whorl of chilled air trembled round Joyce like a portent, catching her breath and wrapping her arms around her bosom.

In the afternoon, the way things happen, out of sorts since the morning, Joyce found herself face to face with the 'babe' across the no-man's-land of the library information desk. Oh yes, the young men had not been wrong—annoyingly luxurious hair in some sort of elaborate braid, long slim body, loud confident attitude. 'I'd like to apply for a Trinity library pass to help me with my research,' said Delilah, in an irritatingly precious sort of way which suggested that research probably wasn't something the Irish knew a lot about. Joyce, scanning the application, found herself wanting to kill her, while breathing in deeply through her nose and managing to communicate in a sort of strangled gasp, 'I see you've got Professor O'Hara as your tutor.'

'Oh yeah,' gushed Delilah, 'isn't he something?'

'Isn't he just.' Joyce pushed the air out through her teeth.

That night, as Professor O'Hara and his wife shared a fine bottle of Chablis (something they tended to do regularly since he'd become head of the English Department at the university), his wife remarked in her by-the-way voice: 'I hear there's an "American babe" called Delilah in first year.' James, who had had a good look at Delilah during the freshers' induction meeting that morning and made sure she was in his tutorial group, developed a sudden interest in the small print on the wine bottle, while replying casually, 'Oh there's always a fair sprinkling of "babes", as you put it, in first year, although I must say there's a particular energy about this first year lot, quite invigorating for the department really.'

'Hmmm,' responded Joyce, drily, as she regarded her husband of thirty years, the charming James O'Hara, father of their son and daughter, possessed of an incisive intellect, a midlife crisis and a ponytail. She thought of Milan Kundera and his theory about chance happenings, amazing coincidences; fortuities, he called them. Joyce was fascinated by the idea of coincidence, loved pondering on the degree of chance required to link people and events together. She and James had themselves been fatefully drawn together by the magnetic combination of their names, meeting as they had at a Bloomsday celebration; he, rakish in Joycean hat and glasses, she drawing his eye in voluptuous Molly Bloom muslin—an age ago that all seemed now. Her mind wandered to the coincidence of the birth of their daughter Eudora on the same day as Chelsea Clinton. Joyce now felt an affinity with Bill (he pacing in Little Rock while she laboured in Holles Street) which vindicated her staunch defence of him when he was behaving like a prick.

... but then all men were pricks at some time or another, were they not?... forgetting they had wives, carried away by some young one with chutzpah and looks... and if they were charming enough they got away with it... ah yes, fortuity, coincidence, fate, call it what you will, but of all the English departments in all the universities in all the world a babe called Delilah has to walk into my husband's.

Joyce O'Hara sensed a fortuity of immense proportions gathering force around her. Her pet name for her husband was Samson.

She thought nobody else knew about the nickname, but of course, this being Ireland, and, in particular, a small university town, everybody did. Delilah, hearing the name whispered to her at the freshers' induction meeting by a first year repeat called Alice, had also a sensation of being sucked into a fortuitous moment in time—how could she not? For there was more than the mythical pairing of the names Samson and Delilah; there was the fact that the name Delilah was also a nickname, acquired some years earlier at a student party in Boston College when she had taken the scissors to a drunk and offensive young male and cut his hair off while he slept. She could, of course, have discarded this name when she came to Ireland, and had been in half a mind to revert to her real name, which was Anna, but found herself changing her mind the moment she laid eyes on the interesting Professor O'Hara of the ponytail and enigmatic eyes. When she was introduced to him as Delilah Barrymore from Boston, a young writer who would be attending English classes as an occasional student for the coming academic year, they shook hands almost mischievously and afterwards neither could remember who raised an eyebrow first.

Professor James O'Hara was well aware of the virtues and failings attributed to him by his wife, but he was even more acutely aware of the sexual attraction he held for many of his female students, who gazed at him and blushed and were awkward in his presence. He realised this was in part due to the student worship phenomenon which seemed to apply even if a lecturer looked like a horse's arse. In his case, however, it was in no small way, he felt, due to his innate sexuality and to his voice, achingly rich, he had been told, which he allowed to rise, then to fall almost to a whisper, so that students leaned towards him in the lecture hall in a half swoon of intimacy as he intoned on wastelands and worms and roses. That Delilah should be attracted to him was therefore not in itself surprising, but the Samson-Delilah coincidence could not but strike him as ironic and rather alarming. When Joyce called him Samson he quite naturally assumed a connection with Milton's *Samson Agoniste*, all strength and pillars and teasing metaphors, but the more vulgar tale of Samson having his locks cut off by a scheming Delilah was a different kettle of fish altogether, considering his attachment to his beloved ponytail. For his grey-gold ponytail was not just about a refusal to let go of his youth; it had become, in fact, central to his image, striking others, he imagined, as an artistic counterpoint to the elegance of his academic gown, a garment which he affected to wear each day, much to the annoyance of his colleagues in the Arts faculty.

The first time she came to him in his room he was overcome by a bleakness, a sense of a foreshadowing of intense possibility which it would be up to him to include in or reject from his life. She had come to him straight from a lecture in which he had read, rather beautifully, he thought, from Muldoon's 'Incantata,' the intimate love poem which begins: 'I thought of you tonight, *a leanbh*...'

'What does "a leanbh" mean?' she asked him, and he replied, 'Darling,' knowing quite well that it did not, but unable to stop himself, the word hanging between them as if no further words were necessary, or even possible.

And neither did it seem possible that they would not be drawn towards each other into a fictive world of desire; these two, the teacher past his youth, seeped in an imaginary world of words and language, and the young aspiring writer, honing her craft on the waves of make-believe. Their narrative was played out against the backdrop of first year English literature, across a sea of literary love that had never been or would never be again: Yeats, who would never be loved by Maud Gonne; Gretta Conroy grieving for her young lover, Michael Furey, in 'The Dead.' What chance did they have in a climate of literary criticism where sexual politics played such a pivotal role, where every sigh was analysed, every glance deconstructed, tutorials informed by the whisper of angels dancing on the heads of pins.

After tutorials, which were held in his room, he would sometimes say, 'May I have a word, Delilah?' and the other students, banished, would convulse with laughter in the corridor outside. 'A word, yeah *right*, is that what he calls it?' And later that night across the Student Union someone would call, 'Hi Tom, I suppose a word would be out of the question?'

But that was all it was—words. Rivulets of words, pools of words, words spoken and unspoken, half-whispered, half-heard. He would say quietly to her, 'And how is our work in progress?' and instead of the smart rejoinder she longed to make she would find herself leaning into her bag, retrieving pages from her latest short story. He admired her writing, liked its fluidity and lyricism but thought her style too reminiscent of Virginia Woolf and encouraged her to allow her own voice to emerge. He warned about overuse of interior monologue and a formlessness of character which he detected in her work. She expected him to kiss her, and was surprised and disappointed when he didn't, but the stream of students past his window plus muffled noises from the corridor were reminders that discretion must prevail. He would come from behind his desk to find a book on his cluttered shelves and they would stand hip to hip, heads almost touching, hands not quite reaching, in a pose of unfulfilled desire, discussing a passage from Carver or Hemingway. Students passing the window, very slowly, it must be noted, reported seeing them like this, or sitting at his desk, a book between them, not reading, or talking, but simply gazing at each other. These reports varied, depending on the time of night or how often the story had been retold; memory played tricks, and in an atmosphere of Chinese whispering the only thing the students agreed on was that, whatever this thing was between Samson and Delilah, if they could bottle it they'd make a fortune.

The faculty was agog with speculation; students drank their coffee by day and their beer by night in a warm belonging of gossip; the staff watched with amusement tempered by anxiety. At times Delilah was surrounded by a small group of friends, mostly roommates from the student residence where she lived, the students hoping for some confidence, some titbit which they could proudly whisper next day. But when Alice would say, 'Ah c'mon Delilah, what's the story with yourself and Samson?' Delilah would toss her hair and say, 'Story, what story? There *is* no story.' But she liked the idea of a narrative developing around herself and James O'Hara, the sense that they had been assigned roles in the remake of *Samson and Delilah*, the ending not yet written.

As the winter drew in it seemed to Delilah that the beginning had scarcely been written. Sometimes she thought she imagined the whole thing, that her writer's mind had conjured up something which did not in fact exist. She was often solitary, walking under the dark trees of the deserted campus on a December evening, over the bridge towards the lights of the 'dreaming spire' of the old chapel, half hoping she would meet him, although she never did.

On one such walk, her feet freezing, pellets of icy sleet catching her breath, she began to reflect that what had started out as a mischievous game had somehow, for her, metamorphosed into something much more. She was humiliated by the fact that he had never suggested meeting her outside of the academic timetable. She had expected they would be lovers by now, the thing between them running its course, burning itself out.

She passed under the dark shadow of the Aula Maxima and into the square of the old campus, history surrounding her, casting, it seemed to her, a cold eye on her misery. He had mentioned a Yeats' weekend in the new year. Did he mean they would be together then? And after that, what then? She felt out of control, her confidence sapped, fearful she might lose this game which was no longer a game, cursing the weird selection programme that had thrown them together, finally admitting to herself that she had fallen for him, the bastard.

Through the gates of the university and up into the small town, the warmth of the student pub luring her, all noise and bursts of laughter and discordant Christmas carols, but proving no match for the words and phrases forming and splintering in her head; her sense of dislocation acute; her thoughts turning on alternatives… *shatter this ridiculous myth, forget the name Delilah, my name is Anna, go home, go home to Boston…* she turned suddenly, tears freezing in the fur of her hood, almost savouring the foolishness, the timelessness of her situation, a rich store of emotions settling in her consciousness, the need to transfer her thoughts to paper bringing her swiftly to her rooms.

The O'Haras, meanwhile, sip *Pouilly Fumé* in their warm, lamplit drawing room. James is restless, finding excuses to return to the college, half hoping he will meet her, although he never does. Joyce never mentions Delilah again. She dresses elegantly and with great care, in silk and linen, her blonde bob sleek and shining, her eyes inchoate, her talk bright. From time to time sniggers of whispered conversation waft towards her in the library: '...wonder has Delilah her scissors sharpened yet... What will the Prof look like without his ponytail...'

Delilah herself drifts across her vision now and then—statuesque, beautiful, in expensive jeans and short sweaters, eyes avoiding, knowing quite well who Joyce is.

In the library one January morning a poster is hung, advertising the Yeats Weekend Winter School in Sligo. *Members of Professor O'Hara's tutorial group interested in attending please contact the Secretary of the English Department as soon as possible.*

In the end all ten members of the tutorial group elect to go, as if each fears he or she will miss too much if they stay away. Although the weekend trip has been set up by the Professor, precisely so that he and Delilah may be together, of necessity it must take on the semblance of a jolly, instructive student outing—the Professor hoping the other lecturers will think 'how sporting of old O'Hara to take a crowd of first years to Sligo' while knowing damn well they would think no such thing.

Both packed with seduction in mind; Delilah purchasing delicate silk camisoles and French knickers; James escaping from a seminar at Trinity to select a velvet smoking jacket which he felt might be just the sartorial touch required for quiet drinks in his room—he allowed himself to think no further than that. As he closed his bag on Friday afternoon Joyce handed him a pair of scissors, 'just in case the hair might need a trim.'

In the Sligo Park Hotel as the Yeats Winter School got underway, Delilah, seeing James O'Hara with his colleagues and counterparts from other universities, was struck by the hierarchy in which she found herself; to these professors, lecturers, poets and writers she was but a student expected to bow to their gravitas; indeed, had she been less self-absorbed she would have realised that the hierarchy operated inside the academic circle as well and that many a feather would be ruffled before the weekend was over. Her professor was kind, but of necessity drawn into another world of scholarship, a world which had been earned by long years of lecturing, publishing and occasional back-stabbing.

From the other side of the room she watches him spend time with Ireland's smiling laureate, Hamish Sheeney, discussing arrangements for the following night when James will give a short poetry reading before the great man's lecture on 'Yeats and Love.' She hears Joyce's name mentioned frequently as she is enquired after, 'Give her my love, must get together soon, how are Eudora and Tobias?' *Eudora and Tobias—Christ, how pretentious!*

She felt exhausted, alienated, turned back on the students to whom she had paid so little attention on campus. They include her in their group, magnanimous in her discomfort, the young men and women pleased for different reasons. After the musical interlude which follows the welcoming address by the President of the Yeats Society she finds herself seated beside a young Ph.D. student from Queen's University who talks enthusiastically about his thesis on the healing effect of literature on the troubled North. She hears herself telling him distractedly about her interest in writing, about ideas she has for some new short fiction. She notices James being swept away by the organising committee, hears talk of checking out the Yeats Memorial Building, cars starting up outside, doors banging shut.

At Lissadell next day, after a night of stormy dreams and waves lashing the Sligo coast, he seeks out Delilah. He finds her, in Yeatsian pose, almost as he had expected: her hand on the round polished table, the light from the great windows open to the south, her beauty gazelle-like. He watches her, his thoughts fragmenting as they had done in his dream last night. He sees her as Maud Gonne, haughty, denying, morphing into Delilah, astride Samson with scissors in her hand, himself, reaching out, calling to two lovers called James and Anna, whom he can't reach, who can't hear him through the storm and the crashing waves. He thinks he might be going a little mad. He notices the attention she is being paid by that young fellow Sean from Belfast, *brilliant scholar, so they say, good-looking, have to admit, in an annoying Pierse Brosnan sort of way,* and does not immediately turn her head when he speaks to her.

'Are you enjoying the weekend?' he asked her quietly.

'Yes indeed, most instructive'

He studied her. 'A drink with me tonight in my room?'

She almost leaned into him, and in truth, if she had done so he would hardly have resisted. Instead, she inclined her head slightly and taking that for assent, he nodded, but before he could continue he found himself being addressed by a persistent junior lecturer from UCC who was after a job in his department. The junior lecturer would wonder for the rest of his life why he did not get the job when he was clearly the most qualified candidate.

At dinner that night he sits at table with the academics, she with the other students. Among his own kind he is different, imposing a foolishness upon her which it is humiliating to acknowledge. Before she came here she had imagined she would sit by his side. She wears a stunning dress of midnight blue, zipped down the back of the strapless bodice, her hair falling to her waist. She blushes into her wild salmon and turns her head to acknowledge a remark from Sean. As James O'Hara rises to speak Sean seems to be inviting her to Queen's for a seminar with Eoin McNamee, the Northern writer whose dream-like prose she greatly admires. 'You'll find it wonderfully refreshing, so you will, postmodern writing at its best after all this Yeats stuff—very good for your own writing.'

She listened to the familiar voice reading the familiar lines; holding her gaze as he 'murmured a little softly how love fled and paced upon the mountains overhead and hid her face amid a crowd of stars'; heard him segue into 'things fall apart, the centre cannot hold' and a warning bell chimed in her soul and it seemed as if her spirit left her body and floated high in space, looking down upon the scene below. She saw the two of them from a great distance, their faces and bodies in mist, two dreamers whom fate had teased to a madness, seduced by the fantasy of a myth. Samson and Delilah. She watched as the mist wafted their story away from them, and all the love they could have known drifted away, engulfing them in an aura of incredible bleakness. She heard a chair scraping backwards and realised it was her own, as she stood and went from the room, and in the echo of her footsteps she could hear the laughter of the gods and their whispers, 'Where is the drama, the myth must end in drama.'

And James O'Hara, watching her, at one with her in the epiphany of that moment, sensed also that it was over. As he left the podium to applause for Sheeney he knew that their story would end here tonight, with what consequences he didn't dare to imagine. He climbed the stairs and entered his room and Delilah followed him; there was no velvet smoking jacket, no removal of a midnight-blue dress. He held her and she held him and they both said 'Darling' and meant it. But the story could not be over till Delilah wielded the scissors, as she had always known she must (what irony that they should be Joyce's scissors, waiting in that room as if she herself had placed them there), for the gods must be appeased and the myth must have its ending. James O'Hara gasped as clouds of hair fell to the floor and kept on falling, then bent and caught a soft black tendril and closed it, for eternity, in the palm of his hand.

Delilah stayed longer in Belfast than she had intended; it suited her, this dear old city; made her feel like she'd been there before. Its images and contradictions appealed to her; the atavistic mindset and dark beauty of the old streets juxtaposed with a leafy modernity and a dry humour and warmth. She had been easily accepted into Sean's world in the postgrad community of Queen's where she would return shortly to take up a place in the graduate school of creative writing. She was fragile, different, but felt a promise within her that she might find a niche among the new generation of Northern writers finding their voice in the wake of the troubles. As to her old life, the laughter of the gods had faded, and for James O'Hara there had been no loss of face. Her hair became her, as she had known it would.

When she returned, briefly, to the university in the small town, Delilah went first to the library to work on her latest fiction; it would turn on the themes of hubris, desire and ambiguity.

Joyce watched her, the soft blue velvet beret elegant on the dark cropped head.

'What really happened in Sligo?' Joyce wondered. 'What sacrifices were made, and by whom?'

'What happened to Delilah's hair?' the students whispered.

But Delilah wasn't talking, and, needless to say, neither were the O'Haras.

XAVIER, 1995
Nuala Ní Chonchúir

YOU ARRIVED IN BARCELONA WITH NO PLAN other than to experience it. In your head it was a gothic place, all teetering Gaudiesque towers and endless nights. The reality of it wasn't too different: the maze of laneways off the Ramblas pumped their dark sensuality like a medieval carnival, night and day, and there was a vibrancy to the roaming crowds of rich and poor. Barcelona didn't wear the pristine frilliness of Germanic cities, it had its own dirty-sweet, lived-in charm, like a treasured vintage dress. The Gaudi buildings weren't everywhere, as you had expected, but the place was beautiful and unlike any other you'd been in. Arriving in October, you found the city still basking under summer's heat and you were glad of it, after a rainy Dublin September.

The studio you rented was in El Raval, overlooking a busy laneway that was chock-a-block with cheap Indian restaurants. It took two months for you to adjust your body to the rhythms of the neighbourhood: quiet mornings, noisy nights. The women in the flat opposite—there were five of them and two small babies—were performers, seamstresses or prostitutes: spangled, sequiny costumes lounged on rows of wall-hooks, or sat in their laps for mending. You could lie in your bed by the window and look across the alley, through the railings of the balcony, into their flat. They may have been Cuban: they shimmied and shuffled together every afternoon to Latino music, swinging the children in their arms occasionally and shouting at each other constantly.

Five days a week you pulped fruit and vegetables into long glasses for thirsty tourists. Seven nights a week you played with your new friends: a gaggle of Aussies, Catalans and Brits, with the odd Kiwi thrown into the mix for flavour. Xavier—beautiful, angry Xavier—was a native. You met him, ridiculously, in an Irish bar called The Ramblers. Like most Irish abroad, you flocked to the Guinness sign when it presented itself in your first week in the city. The workers in the bar were all English, the beer was twice the price of everywhere else, but the music was from home and it was comforting, some nights, to hear familiar accents.

You had spotted Xavier early on in the evening; he didn't look like any other Catalan you'd met. He wore a raggy T-shirt, his head was dirty with stubble and he looked belligerent and unhappy. But he was watching you, just as you couldn't stop watching him. Chatting with your workmates, you flicked your eyes in his direction from time to time and he stared back. It was late when he came up behind you at the bar and wound his hand into your hair, like a snake.

'Your hair is like ashes.'

'Is that a compliment?'

'Yes,' he said, but pronounced it '*jess*'. He asked if you were from Ireland and when you said that you were, he just nodded.

'Are you from Barcelona?'

'Near here.'

You leaned your head back off the end of the bed; the balcony door was open to let what small breeze might be blowing in through the studio. The ceiling fan was frozen again—it gave off an eerie whine that sounded like cats in heat. With your eyes half shut, the green ceiling-rose seemed to shiver and spin. Xavier was sucking at your throat, pumping your breasts between his hands and grunting with each thrust he made. Sweat slid from his thighs to yours, from his belly to yours. His long body cleaved onto you in a perfect way. Like he said, you were a fit. Your neck was sore from holding it back over the hard edge of the mattress; you opened your eyes fully. The Latino women were watching you and Xavier: they had gathered on their balcony, and they languished there, staring at your heaving bodies as if they were looking at a film on TV.

You locked your eyes onto the eyes of the eldest woman, the one you had christened Rosa because of her china-doll red cheeks. She fanned her face with a magazine, then raised one eyebrow at you. You smiled, lifted your head and kissed Xavier deeply, forcefully. He said he was going to come and you matched his jutting and urged him on until he released himself into you with his familiar whimper. You kissed wetly, for a long time, and when you looked across the alley again, the women were gone.

Xavier rolled a joint for the two of you to share and you sat up in the bed, watching his nimble fingers skin, flame, crumble, roll and light. It would've taken you ten minutes to do it, so you were glad he was rolling and not you. He offered you the first drag and the smoke hit the back of your throat like pepper. You breathed long on its heat again, then handed it to him.

'You know, in Ireland we pronounce your name *Ecks-save-yer*. Or some people just say *Save-yer*.'

He snorted, blowing smoke through his nose in ragged puffs. 'Say that again. Ecks-something?'

'Ecks-save-yer. It's terrible, isn't it? *Ecks-save-yer, come in for your dinner, it's gettin' cauld.*' You laughed. 'The way you say it is just so much sexier. *Xav*ier. Xavi*er*.'

'I like your name too. Lillis. It's pretty. What does it mean?'

'Oh, it's just the flower, the lily. It's Greek. My mother has absurd taste—she called my poor brother Robin, like the bird, and he's this enormous, grizzly thing.'

Xavier pressed his hand into your stomach, rubbing at the mingled sweat that was still gathered there. You loved the look of his honey-brown skin, with its lattice of tattoos, against your body which stubbornly stayed pale as milk.

'I wish I had a tan,' you said.

'I like your skin,' he fingered your shoulder, 'it's like the inside of a turnip.' Your face must have dropped. 'I mean that in a good way,' he added, smiling, and he kissed your nose. You touched the raised veins on his inner arms; they were as darkly blue as a tracery of rivers on a vellum map.

'You're so gorgeous, Xavier.'

He leaned over and kissed you, long and lovingly. The smoke had made you both sluggish and his tongue felt thick and welcome against yours.

In Café Alex you ate bruise-tipped asparagus spears, pimentos that were both smoky and sweet, and beef tomatoes slick with olive oil. Xavier poked at his dish with a cocktail stick—every so often stabbing a piece of feta or a glossy green olive—and swigged mightily at a bottle of beer. Night had closed down fast over the city; Xavier looked at his watch, said he had to meet someone about something. He was jittery and seemed angry again but you were afraid to ask who he was meeting and why. You gulped at your wine and talked about the letter your brother had sent, all about the new boy he'd met and how he thought this one was 'the one'.

'As usual,' you said and smiled, thinking of Robin. A sudden compassion for him welled out of nowhere and you realised you were missing him a lot. 'Robin's great, you know? We get on well, more like friends than brother and sister; I can really talk to him.' Xavier barely lifted his eyes to show he was listening, so you shut up and concentrated on eating. It was late and this was the first meal you'd had all day.

'Let's go,' he said.

'I'm still eating.'

'Just hurry up.'

'I don't want to hurry up, I've loads left.' You pointed at the various *tapas* dishes ranged around your plate. Xavier stood and hovered over the table clicking his fingers, in an absent, urgent way. In the end, you slugged back your wine and stuffed the last of your food into your mouth; a slew of oil rilled down your chin and you wiped it away as you followed him out onto Plaça Reial.

The square was heaving with people: open-air diners, buskers, jugglers, wanderers and tourists. You stopped, looked around and spotted Marina, the small girl from London who often came into the café you worked in. You waved, but she looked like she was off her head: her eyes were closed and she was playing a tin-whistle; her head lolled and she lurched from table to table, begging for a few *pesetas*. A huge-armed man with a cluster of dreads at the nape of his neck stayed near her, watching, never letting her stray too far. Looking at him watching Marina made you feel sick. Turning around, you realised that Xavier was gone, lost in the mill of people on the square.

You were a little drunk and you didn't like the idea of having to walk the dim alleyways alone. Running into the middle of Plaça Reial, you hoped to see Xavier ahead of you, but you scanned the crowds and didn't find him. You walked quickly up a narrow street, nearly tripping over two people who were sprawled on the ground in the dark. The night's heat gathered around your face and your upper lip began to dampen; you folded your arms around your body, dipped your head and ploughed through the people walking towards you. Then, realising that you probably looked agitated, you slowed your pace and stepped more surely; you were glad to see the lit-up markets stalls of the Ramblas ahead. Hearing someone running behind you, you turned to see Marina coming up the alleyway. She was clutching the tin-whistle and her bag of coins; she banged into you and grabbed at your arm.

'Please, please, help me. You know me, you know me,' she babbled. Her eyes were rolling in their sockets and she looked feverish, but her clutching hand was strong on your arm. You told her to calm down and glanced behind to see if her dreadlocked minder was coming after her.

'Marina! Marina! It's me, it's Lillis,' you said, shaking her. She seemed to be asleep on her feet. 'Can you run?'

She nodded, her head bobbing like a toddler's, so you dragged her, half-running, up the alley to the Ramblas. Once there, you weaved through people and crossed the road into El Raval, then took a roundabout route to your studio on Carrer de Sant Pau, where you shoved her up the stairs ahead of you.

You woke to a rhythmic pounding on the door. When you opened your eyes, you saw the back of Marina's short dirty-blonde hair beside you on the pillow and couldn't figure out why she wasn't Xavier. The wheening of the ceiling fan blended with the thumping that went on and on. You remembered what had happened.

'Who is it?'

'It's me. Who do you think it is?'

You let Xavier in.

'Where the hell did *you* get to?' He saw Marina on the bed, still dressed in worn ski-pants and T-shirt. 'What the fuck is she doing here?'

'She had nowhere to go.'

'Get her out of here, she's a dirty junkie.'

'She's only a kid.'

'Get her *out*! She's a fucking pro,' he shouted.

'Keep your voice down, Xavier. This is my place and I'm letting her stay.'

'Do you have any idea who her pimp is, Lillis?'

You shook your head.

'It's French Bernard. Do you know him?'

'I've seen him. Big. Dreadlocks.'

'You don't want to make an enemy of that man, believe me, Lillis. I should know.'

'What could I do? She just needed a little help.'

'For your own sake, and mine, get rid of her.' Xavier was pointing his finger into your face. You pushed it away.

'She's staying.'

He let a roar and kicked at the leg of a chair, sending it skidding across the tiles; it crashed into the wall. Marina didn't even stir.

'Lillis, make a choice: if she stays, I go.'

You looked at him, at the raw anger that tensed his whole body. Then you looked at Marina, curled on the bed like a baby.

'I think you'd better leave.'

Xavier threw up his arms. 'You crazy bitch.' He turned away, then swung back, went to say something and stopped himself; he crossed the floor, opened the door and looked at you.

'Thank you, fuck you, and good bye.' The slamming door made you wince.

'Goodbye, Xavier,' you said to the air.

Marina sat up, rubbed at her eyes. You smiled at her. 'How are you doing? Breakfast?'

She stood up out of the bed, reached for her whistle and bag. 'I have to go and find Bernard,' she said, 'he'll be looking for me.'

'Wait, Marina.' You put your hand on her shoulder. 'Will you be okay? Will Bernard not be angry with you for running off?'

Marina shrugged. 'Thanks, Lillis. For the bed. See you around, yeah?'

You let her go.

Holding Hands

David Albahari

Translated from the Serbian by Ellen Elias-Bursac

WE GAVE A PARTY ON THURSDAY. There were seven married couples invited, several divorced women and men, and four of my wife's students. My wife teaches physics and chemistry to recent immigrants, those who want further training or a change of vocation in order to fit into the system of the country they have chosen as their new home. We told everyone to come at around 8pm, and by 8.30 there was such a ruckus in the house that our cat didn't dare poke its nose out of the closet it had crawled into when the first guests knocked at the door. The last to come, a Japanese couple, arrived at nine. They bowed for ages at the door and apologised for coming late, but in the end I did manage to steer them into the house. I also managed to figure out what they'd like to drink—she wanted tomato juice and he asked for a beer—and after I had introduced them around to the people standing near us, I went off to find clean glasses. I opened the kitchen door, and there, in the middle of the room, stood my wife and a dark-skinned man, and they were holding hands.

'Ah,' said my wife, 'you got here just at the right time. This is Ahmed.'

They kept holding hands and, as far as I could see, they had no intention of letting go.

'Ahmed is my student,' said my wife.

Ahmed said nothing.

'Haruki and Hiroko have arrived,' I said, 'but there are no clean glasses left in the living room.'

'In the dining room cupboard there are clean glasses,' my wife said. She turned and looked at Ahmed through half-closed eyes.

She had never, as long as I could remember, looked at me like that. Her eyes were always either wide open or completely shut, and her eyelids never fluttered just for me.

'What are you waiting for?' my wife asked. 'Didn't you hear me say that there are glasses in the cupboard?'

'Maybe I should bring Ahmed something to drink,' I said, 'if he says what it is he'd like to drink.'

'Ahmed doesn't drink,' my wife said.

There was no longer any reason to linger. I headed toward the dining room. Along the way I plucked two grapes from a bowl sitting on the dishwasher. Before I left, I turned to look back. My wife and Ahmed were still holding hands. I could picture them in a flowery meadow, with the huge orange orb of the sun sinking beyond the horizon. An evening breeze fluttered my wife's floral skirt and billowed Ahmed's green shirt. There were probably some birds there somewhere too. I imagined the bench I was sitting on while watching all this. Then I closed the kitchen door.

'Where is my beer?' asked Haruki with a grin, and added that Hiroko had changed her mind, and she would have a little red wine. 'Red wine is nice,' said Haruki. 'Like bitter chocolate,' added Hiroko. There was a mirror at the back of the shelf, and when I reached for the glasses I thought I might touch my face. It was the glasses, instead, that I touched: a tall straight one for Haruki, and one for wine, perched stork-like on one leg, for Hiroko. Both of them bowed at the same time, and turned to the table with the drinks. I closed the cupboard door and leaned toward the kitchen door. There was no sound.

Haruki and Hiroko came last to the party, and I assume this was why they stayed longer than everyone else did. The act of bidding farewell by our front door took nearly half an hour. First we bowed to one another a few times, then Hiroko gave several compliments on the wine she had sipped, then Haruki gave a five-minute congratulatory oration on the rolls my wife had prepared for the guests, then my wife twice recited the recipe for the fruit tart Hiroko had enjoyed, and Hiroko slowly repeated it back to her, claiming she would remember it and that she had a photogenic memory. Photographic, said Haruki, and bowed to her. Yes, said Hiroko, I have a photographic photogenic memory, and once I've heard something, no matter what it is, I never forget it. How many eggs, I asked, go into the cake? None, said Hiroko, and bowed to me. Maybe it is better if we shake hands, said my wife. She yawned and her teeth flashed in the light of the lamp over the door. Haruki took her proffered hand and bowed. If we keep this up, I said, we'll still be bowing at dawn. Good night, I said, and kissed Hiroko on the cheek.

We waited for their car to pull away, and then we went into the house. Everywhere, on every available surface, there were glasses, small plates, crumpled napkins, trays and bowls. Bits of rolls crunched under foot. The bottles on the table were empty; there was only some of the vermouth left. I began to collect the glasses and plates and put them in the dishwasher. My wife went to the bathroom, and a few minutes later I heard her brushing her teeth. Afterwards there was nothing to hear until she flushed the toilet.

'Someone smoked weed in the bathroom,' she said when she came back into the kitchen, 'and forgot their joint on the edge of the bathtub.'

'That's not fair,' I said. 'It is only decent to ask the host if he minds, and offer him the first hit.'

'Maybe that is how it was back in your day,' my wife said, 'when there were other ways of doing things.'

'Such as,' I hurried to say, 'that a wife holds hands with another man in front of her husband.'

'I knew it,' said my wife. 'I can guess how that must have gnawed at you all evening. Come on, Ahmed is my student!'

'What is that supposed to mean?' I asked, 'I didn't see you holding hands with your other students.'

'There wasn't time,' she said.

'Of course there wasn't,' I replied, 'when you didn't let go of his hand even once.'

'That's not true,' my wife protested. 'Svetlana, my student from Russia, held his hand for a while.'

'Only one of them,' I said, 'his left, because you wouldn't relinquish his right.'

'Do you mean to say,' my wife said, 'that you spent the whole evening fixated on my hands? No wonder the guests felt you were neglecting them.'

'If there was someone being neglected this evening,' I said, 'it was me.'

'Next time I'll tell Ahmed to hold your hand,' my wife answered, 'maybe then you'll feel better.'

She left the kitchen and went to the bedroom. I heard her click on the lamp on the bedside table, turn down the bedspread and get ready to lie down in bed. I waited for her to turn off the light, walked once more through the rooms where the guests had been. Behind the potted cactuses I found two glasses and took them to the kitchen. I shook some food into a bowl for the cat, poured fresh water into another. I called, 'Kitty,' softly, 'kitty, kitty.' She didn't come. She had probably already crawled under the blanket, snuggled up to my wife and was sniffing her hands. I sat on a chair and lowered my head to the table. I leaned first my forehead on the table, then touched my left cheek to the smooth surface, then my right cheeck, and then I fell asleep.

When I opened my eyes, I saw my wife. She was sitting across from me, her hair all tousled, and there was steam rising from the cup that was in front of her. I looked at the window and saw that it was already daytime.

'You spent the whole night here,' my wife said, 'as if you are homeless.'

I shrugged, and winced at the ache in my stiff neck.

'I cannot believe,' my wife said, 'that you got so worked up about what was just a friendly little gesture.'

'A friendly little gesture,' I said, 'that lasted for hours.' I meant my voice to sound sarcastic, but it cracked and squeaked, as if my tongue couldn't manouvere in my parched mouth.

'There is something you should know about Ahmed to help you understand,' my wife said.

She clasped the cup with both hands, the way she did in wintertime, longing for warmth, or the way, of course, she had clasped Ahmed's hand the night before.

'Ahmed is from Iraq,' my wife said, 'and a few days ago he learned that his sister and her children were killed in the bombing.'

She looked me straight in the eyes.

I didn't know whether I could believe her. I asked, 'How many children did she have?'

'Three,' my wife said, and blinked. 'That is why we decided,' she continued, 'that all of us would care for him, to help him deal with the loss more easily.' She smiled and raised the cup to her lips.

'What are you drinking?' I asked.

'Tea,' said my wife. She licked her lips and set the cup on the table.

I reached out and and covered her hand, warm from the warmed cup, with mine. My wife sighed, softly, and then the two of us stared at our hands, pale in contrast to the dark surface of the table. I could feel the blood pulsing through one of them, but I wasn't sure which.

A little while later my wife slowly slipped her hand out and, without a word, brushed away the curls of hair that had slipped onto her face, got up and left the kitchen. I heard her open the wardrobe in the bedroom, probably looking for the clothes she would wear that day at school. I imagined her standing in front of the blackboard and writing out chemical formulae. Sitting at the desks behind her, the students are diligently copying everything from the blackboard into their notebooks. Only Ahmed is not writing. Instead he is staring at his open palm, as if reading his fate from the pale lines sketched across the darker skin.

I lifted my hand, picked up my wife's cup and had a sip of the tea. The tea was tepid and bitter from having steeped for too long. It could use a few spoonfuls of sugar, I thought. I shifted my weight, drew my feet from under the chair, but I didn't get up. I saw the sugar bowl on the shelf over the stove, and the spoon was lying right by it. A step, maybe two, was all I'd need to reach them. I closed my eyes and slowly dropped my head to the table again. Somewhere inside me, somewhere very far away, I saw an airplane winging off, bombs dropping from under its wings, flaming tongues rising high into the air. I heard our front door open and shut. Then silence ruled in the house. A while later the cat miaowed, but no matter how much I called to it and peered into all its hiding places, I couldn't find it.

Avenging the Stilts Man
Colin O'Sullivan

THIS HAPPENED TO TONY C. He was sitting drinking espresso minding his own business, when he saw a man on stilts. Now, you may think all guys on stilts look ridiculous. But not in Tony C's eyes. He likes the cut of them. Thinks it an art. To be up that high and walking straight, waving at the little kiddies as they try to figure it all out, now that's accomplishment.

Tony waves to the man on stilts. The stilts man waves back.

Then the most bizarre thing happens. The stilts man stumbles a bit, gets his head caught in overhead electric wires, starts spinning round, long legs buckling and gyrating like the blades of a drunk helicopter, his top hat falls off, and he falls bang down on his face.

Blood pours out from the eyes of the stilts man.

This isn't funny according to Tony C. Not one bit.

People form a circle. Amazing how quick people are to form a circle when a body is found or when someone has an epileptic fit, and yet no one lends a hand. Good job Tony is on the scene. He rushes to where the circus performer lays long on the ground.

A child wails; the summer tragedy all too much.

Tony shouts for someone to call an ambulance and a young dreadlocked man obliges, flipping open his mobile and yelling into it.

Tony clutches the stilts man's hand.

'It's okay, you're gonna make it.'

It takes all his years of know-how for Tony to keep the whole thing together. Gotta stay calm. And he can't wait too long either, he has to skedaddle before the ambulance arrives, can't be seen by the authorities. Too risky.

Before he does give them all the slip he promises to avenge the wrongs done to the stilts man. The fallen entertainer, confused, searches deep into Tony's eyes.

Avenge what?

But Tony's certain. Someone's gonna pay.

He makes sure to slip his hand inside the jacket and pick out a business card. He knew the guy would have one. Tony has good hunches.

Rick Spears, Stilts Man.

He pats Rick Spears on the cheek. A promising pat. More blood spurts out onto the asphalt.

'Think of me as your guardian angel.'

Then, ambulance siren, and Tony splits.

Many people conjecture as to the real name of Tony C. People pertaining to be in the know will tell you that it is an Italian name, but too damn tricky to pronounce. 'C' is concise, does the job. Tony does have the dark eyes, the dark hair; you could believe he was Italian or Sicilian. Others think it stands for 'crook' or 'cards' (Tony's fondness for poker) or 'carpets' (the prosperous store he owns) and other C words you don't care to say out loud. But Tony likes his simple surname, and he doesn't mind when people speculate, he can't help who he is or the way he was brought up. In the poorer neighborhoods stealing was commonplace, didn't mean to do anybody any harm.

Survival is still what it's all about.

When he left the scene he was upset and nothing could clear his mind of it. Hours later he still felt like weeping, but that didn't look good in Ladbroke's betting office. Although many men must have probably shed buckets of tears in such an emporium, Tony knew not to let emotions show, keep a straight face, always.

'You okay, Tony? You look a little peaky,' says Benny, having shut up shop and popped in to catch the last race at Doncaster.

'Peaky? What's peaky?'

'Dunno. Just how you look.'

'Bad day, Benny. Saw something terrible. Can't get it out of my head. I think I'm going to be busy for the next few days. Got a little project going.'

It was best for Benny not to ask any more. A 'project' meant something underhand, wayward, crooked, something you didn't want to know about. If Tony C wanted to tell you about it he would. And he didn't look like talking about it just then, looked a bit too *peaky*.

Tony rose early the next morning. Decided to pay the Electricity Board a visit. He finished the breakfast his wife Mary cooked; great eggs on toast as usual, had a slurp of coffee, and took his potbelly and short legs off his chair and down the road. It was a fresh day and Tony didn't mind walking, didn't want to be seen in the car these days anyway, too risky, still hadn't gotten around to changing the plates. He stopped in to his local shop and got a paper off Ravi. He'd protected Ravi before, when some bully boys were beefing him up. Tony had stepped in, sorted it out, minimum rough play. Tony's been getting a free *Sun* ever since.

Waltzing straight in and up to the shining counter, Tony came face to face with a thin-lipped secretary adjusting her huge glasses on the bridge of her nose.

'Excuse me, but I'd like to make a few enquiries.'

'Oh yeah. Enquiries about what?'

She should be chewing gum, he thought, make the picture complete.

'About electric power lines.'

'What? What do you wanna know?'

'I wanna know who's responsible?'

'Responsible?'

'Yeah. I wanna know who puts them up in what parts of the city, who orders them to be put up, how they get put up, how long they've been up, in fact I want the entire history of the power lines in the city, since their invention... up to yesterday.'

'Yesterday?'

'Yesterday something happened in the city. Near my neighborhood, in fact. And I have to do an investigation.'

'Are you a policeman?'

'No. I'm a concerned citizen. And I need some answers. This is a very serious issue.'

The secretary glanced at her colleague, gave her a *we're-dealing-with-a-nut* kind of expression. Tony ignored the faces, looked around to see if he could spot anyone that looked vaguely like a manager.

'Manager's away today. He's out on a job. Other side of the city. He can tell you about power lines. Though I doubt you'll get an entire history. People who work can be kind of busy you know. Maybe you should go to a library.'

Tony considered this. A library. Too risky.

'Which side of the city is he? I mean, where, exactly?'

The secretary wrote down the address and Tony smiled a *thank you*. The secretaries gave each other a *there-goes-a-nut*, and an *oh-yeah* face, but Tony didn't catch them. He was on a mission.

Tony rode the bus. He didn't mind doing this. He could hide behind his paper, never get spotted. He liked Page 3's Lauren. Not a patch on yesterday's twenty-one-year-old Hannah, but she was still more than acceptable. He knew that Mary never liked him looking at these girls, so he usually skipped past that page if she was with him. Tony was old-fashioned, knew courtesy. He read about the wars and destruction that was going on in the world and he sighed at the injustice of it all. Sure, he got his hands dirty once in a while, but it was usually for a good cause, helping out a fellow neighbour or something. Well, that was okay. It was the mindless stuff that Tony C didn't care for. He thought again about the stilts man crashing down and he hung his head in despair. How could people allow this to happen? That stilts man probably had a wife and family. Maybe young babies. Triplets! Tony was definitely doing the right thing, conducting this investigation, righting the wrongs. There was a story too about a council house being flooded; but he had only one pair of hands, only two short legs, and right now he was taken up with avenging the stilts man.

Tony followed the directions on the notepaper. He hung around for a while watching the operation. Trucks, lots of guys moving around, hard hats, tools, large sheets of paper.

Tony smoked; it made him less conspicuous.

He was just a guy out for a stroll, checking out the nags in the paper, having a wee puff. He noticed that most of the workers went to one guy for answers and that guy quickly dispatched them all with authority. He was the one Tony wanted. He casually strolled up when he saw several of them sitting with sandwiches and pouring tea from flasks.

Break time. Perfect.

'Excuse me. Are you the boss around here?'

'Yes. You could call me that. I'm overseeing the electrical engineering here. Who are you?'

'I'm a concerned citizen, sir. I'd like to ask you a few questions about power lines in the city.'

The engineer's brow became furrowed. Tony had him worried.

'What do you want to know?'

'Well, yesterday someone got tangled up in your power lines. Looked a bit dangerous from where I was standing.'

'Really? Tangled? How?'

'He was walking along and got his head twisted in a line.'

'What? Walking? What do you mean? Was he on a trampoline or something? That happened once…'

'No. He was on stilts.'

'Oh. Well, was he hurt?'

'Yes. He's in the hospital.'

The engineer still had the furrowed-brow look. Tony had him rattled.

'Did a line come down? Is it down now? Is that the problem?'

'A man's been hurt. That's the problem,' raising his voice a notch, keep the guy in his place.

'Look, mister. No disrespect or anything. I don't know who you are or what you want, but if a guy is walking around on stilts then he should be a bit more careful. Those lines are high enough. We put them up that high because we don't expect anyone to be walking into them.

Even trucks and buses and things aren't that high. Do you see what I mean? They are pretty safe up there. I make sure of that.'

Tony's eyes became narrow. He bit the inside of his cheek trying not to let his anger show. The man continued:

'I'm sorry if your pal got hurt but we've lots of work to do. If there's a line down we'll take note of the address and get a few guys to drive around and fix it immediately. A line down is pretty dangerous. Now if you don't mind.'

Tony slowly backed away. He decided it was better to let it go for now. He was on his own, couldn't take them all; too many of them. If Benny was there he at least had a chance. He winced when he heard a few of them snigger behind his back. Tony would sort things out sooner or later.

Somebody always pays.

His next stop was the hospital. He asked if a man named Rick Spears was admitted yesterday.

Bingo.

Tony took the elevator to the third floor and pulled up a seat.

'Hello, Rick.'

'Hello. Do I know you?'

Tony gave him a wink, 'I'm the guy at the scene. I won't tell you my full name. Just call me Tony.'

'What scene? Oh, yes. I remember your face now. Are you okay?'

'Yeah. Of course I'm okay; you're the one we should be worrying about.'

'Oh, well, that's awfully kind of you to come in and visit, ah, Tony, but I'm doing all right. I had a bit of concussion, that's all. They are keeping me in one more day for observation, just to be sure. Cut my eye a bit too. It's a long way off those things. I ought to be more careful really. All these years at it and I still tumble. No wonder the circuses don't really want me anymore. Hard to get a job as a stilts man these days.'

'You don't worry about that, Rick. Tony here will sort you out.'

There was a moment of silence as Tony looked around the ward. He didn't want to be recognised. He may well have put some of them here.

He kept his head low.

'Are you okay, Tony?'

'Yeah. Listen. I spoke to a few guys who were responsible for this. Been sorting a few things out. It's not all done and dusted yet, but you can count on me.'

'Responsible for what? All I did was fall. There's no one to blame.'

'A man like you don't just fall, Rick. Those power lines, someone's been tampering. Made it *look* like a fall.'

'Look, all that happened was I walking along and waving at the kids and… in fact, I saw you waving at me and I waved back and lost my footing… yeah, now that I think of it I was waving at you. Weren't you drinking coffee in the Brasilia Café?

'I may have been, Rick.'

'Well, there it is then. I waved at you and then I fell. But look, you don't have to feel bad about it. I should stop all this clowning around. I'm getting too old for it anyway.'

Tony's eyes grew narrow. For once he began to let his true emotions show.

'Now you listen here, Rick. You never stop clowning. Do you hear? It's people like you that make this world a better place. You make the little kiddies laugh. You circus people brighten the lives of hundreds of people. You are an important man, Rick Spears. Now, I'm gonna lay low for a day or two. And when the heat dies down Benny and me, we gonna pay a little visit to a certain Mr McGuire.'

'Who's Mr McGuire?'

'He's the guy behind the operation. He's the engineer responsible for putting up power lines all over the city. He's not getting past Tony C, that's for sure. You take care now, Rick, you don't worry about a thing. I'll come in and see you in a few days.'

Rick Spears watched as the little man shuffled out the door. Tony kept his head down and even lifted his *Sun* up so no one could catch a good look at his face.

Tony got the bus home. He checked in on Benny and told him that the project was going well. He might need a bit more muscle over the next few days though. Benny nodded like he was used to, having learned over the years not to roll his eyes anymore. Benny told him that the takings were good and that it was the best month of the year so far. Even the Prince Hotel had finally come and settled their bill. But Tony looked distant. His mind was on other things. How could they put a man like Rick Spears in hospital, how could they let council houses get flooded? Benny said no more but went to lock the door and put the shutters down for the evening.

Bancher's Daughter
Mary O'Donoghue

BANCHER'S DAUGHTER KNOWS HER KNIVES. A chink of pride opens in his heart. He feels it widen, widening fit to split him asunder.

Gud gurl yurself.

Then he rights himself, sitting bolt straight in the chair. He remembers where he is, why he's here. Leather farts gently under him.

The school principal's office is coloured like a mushroom. Pinky-white on the top half of the walls; from waist height down, the pinky-brown of gills. It must've been a classroom at one time. The entire school is a put-together effort. Some classes are held in prefabs. Long pale-blue chalets. Tinderboxes: they'd go up in an instant, if someone had a mind to lay a fire to them.

Bancher had to fight to get his daughter in here, after the business at the convent. Like being fired from a job, stories of expulsion follow a person, getting bigger as they do the rounds.

It was said that Bancher head-butted his boss.

It was said that Bancher's daughter pinned a nun's arm behind her back.

It was said that Bancher came to work one too many times doddery and blood-eyed with drink.

It was said that Bancher's daughter threw a table.

It was said that Bancher was a danger to himself and others on the job.

And Bancher's daughter was said to be a living lighting threat to teachers and pupils. To the buildings themselves.

'Your daughter brought a carpet knife to school, Mr Bancher.'

A carpet knife. Would you credit it? And the easiest thing to buy, too. You could get them for cheap in PoundWorld, ones with flimsy blades that buckled easily and bright-coloured handles. Sold in plastic packets backed with cardboard, the cardboard printed with instructions for safe use. Exactly like you bought toys. Action Men and Barbies and Jedi Knights shackled with twists of wire to the backs of boxes, hanging one in front of the other.

Bancher preferred to think that she went to a hardware shop for the knife, instead of PoundWorld. A hardware shop had a bit of class to it. Pay the extra bit, and you got the best. The chain with the thickest links, sold in feet, however many you wanted. Tile cutters, heavy knife files, boxes of blades.

'We have every reason to believe that your daughter intended to employ this knife at some stage, Mr Bancher. Given what we know of your daughter's history, we are entitled to our assumption.'

Who are the 'we', the 'us' in this outfit, Bancher wonders. They are alone in the office. Sitting at the enormous desk, the principal looks like a child bellied up to a big table. The mahogany desk looks like it might take several men to lift it. He thinks of it being hoisted by six men, they shouldering it like a coffin, and the principal draped along the top of it like one of those blondes on the bonnet of a Ferrari or a Lamborghini. The ones you used to see in posters, those posters that lads framed as expensively, displayed as importantly, as a piece of work in a museum.

But this feat of imagination fails him when he notices that the principal is wearing a brooch at her throat. The ultimate *Don't-you-even-think-about-mentally-undressing-me* weapon. *Cos you'll prick your pretend unbuttoning paws on this savage sharp prong, you will.*

He tries instead to hold her gaze, but feels wilted by the pity he sees there. She feels sorry for him. She thinks that she's breaking some terrible news, some awful bulletin of dysfunction. And that's how it should have been. After all Bancher has done over the last seven or eight years to rise them up in the world. The news that his daughter has brought a carpet knife to school should shaken him, sicken him, make him resolve to work harder. Be an iron fucking fist in her upbringing.

But instead he finds himself sliding his thumb across his bent forefinger, moving an invisible blade forward. Just the sharp snout of it. The merest triangle of metal. Ah, the lovely threat of it rasping the thick skin of his thumb.

'We are loath, however, even under these extreme circumstances, to expel your daughter, Mr Bancher.'

Her sentences are like triple jumps. Landing. Just where. She wants them to.

'We pride ourselves on our progressive attitude to problem pupils.'

Oh yah; he remembers the (P)PPP of the school's manifesto. It was told to him only after he'd had to beg them to take her. He'd begged like a cur for a cronge of bread. He'd made a fool of himself.

And here he is, sitting across from a woman who's just used the word 'loath' in a sentence, and presented him with the good news that she isn't about to give his daughter the boot. She smells of something that he's sprayed into the cap of an aerosol can in Boot's. Limara. They used to have the best ads on television. Half-naked cartoons. A voice ripping off Robert Plant, singing 'I'm gonna wake you... remember my name... Lim-aaa-ra!'

She's going to give a chance to his daughter, his knife-carrying daughter who could've nicked into a carotid artery in quick-time and given the place a right paint show.

'We will, however, see to it that she takes her classes under one-to-one tuition, for a period of one month.'

Two-ition, she says, as an American would pronounce it.

'Because, Mr Bancher, we don't want word of the knife incident causing, shall we say, repercussions among our more volatile pupils.'

He wants to tell her that 'reprisals' would be a better word. It had more of the terrorist about it. Of course, the school can well afford to pay teachers for his daughter's tuition. It's absorbed into the fees he pays three times a year, his hand cramping as he writes the massive cheques.

Bancher thinks that his daughter might be treated like a serial killer for the duration of her punishment. They'd cage her. Give her all the books she wants. But never anything sharp; not so much as a colouring pencil. Knitting would be out of the question. The tutors would have to be trained in self-defence. How to shoot straight if the place was plunged into darkness. Bancher might visit her with a sliver of Gillette's Closest Shave under his tongue. It's a nice thought, like something from a film. He has to force himself to draw back from it and listen to the principal drone on about the school's success with problem pupils. She speaks with the glazed zeal of a Jehovah's Witness telling you how wonderful their book is.

Bancher has to buy into what the principal is selling to him. It's part of his scrubbed-up life. It's a way to keep things alright. Even keel. She's offering him a Plan for Damage Limitation. And Bancher is well up for that.

Bancher can only remember mumbling, 'Thank you, thank you indeed.' He adds the 'indeed' because it seems like the kind of expression she'd appreciate. He thinks he may have even called her 'ma'am'. He backs into the door; he backs out into the corridor; he lays his sweating hands against the cold skin of the wall.

He'd prefer to think that his daughter bought a carpet knife, stowed it in one of the hundred pockets on her army-green canvas bag, because she needed to know that it was there. For protection. For slicing the air with threats to the boys who might be making fun of the birthmark that lay alongside her ear, almost the same length as a sideburn. St Anthony's Fire, as it was called. As if that somehow made it alright. Sanctified it.

Bancher had broached the topic of special concealing cream with her only once, showing her the Before and After pictures in the back pages of a woman's magazine. She'd reacted by telling him not to be so stupid; by saying that it wasn't that big of a deal; by reminding him that her hair mostly covered it. And anyway, she didn't give a shit what people thought.

But Bancher would've preferred that she was being taunted by the most pitiless malicious names for her poor printed face. That she'd bought the knife for backup. That she liked how safe it felt to carry, its blade slid fully into the handle like a snail's head pulled back into its shell. That it was her secret, the power she was biding until someday someone went too far, and she showed them what she had looking out for her.

He would've preferred that to the other possibility. And it was always there, even though he thought he'd escaped it by her being a girl. The chance that she hadn't taken it from the wind, hadn't licked it from the stones.

Chip off the block.

Bad drop.

The thing that was in him, and sent him, back before she was born, looking for thick chain and boxes of blades. Bancher. All six feet of him, tank-shouldered and beered to the gills, making the terraces his own.

Did he like football back then?

Did he hell?

But he loved the crowds it mashed together, and he loved the streets afterwards. Tributaries thick with panicky people, all running from the source. The ones he brought to their knees. Finding the precise hiding place of a kidney, jabbing his boot into that spot beneath the love-handles. He knew, from when he'd been down himself, the way the pain roared like a siren, made you think that dying itself would have to be better than this hot *va-voom* inside you.

And the ones whose faces he branded. Opening smiles on lads' cheeks. When the lips closed on the wounds, the small sickle of skin let everyone know how it had happened. Because everyone with a knife had their own trademark.

Even now, Bancher's throat itches when he watches faces in the stands on television. The camera pans just slowly enough to show their mouths shaping the long loud words of songs. The group has a repertoire for referees, managers, players. Then there's always the impromptu piece, tricked off to a familiar tune, and within two lines the whole gang has it. They love it like a new toy. They laugh after each rendition.

Some fucker ate all the lard.
Some fucker ate all the lard.
Some fucker.
What fucker.
That fucker there.

When Bancher watches these faces on the screen, remembered lines pour into his head, and he can hear the slurry voice closest his ear. The way he felt almost in love with the beery breath, he had that much goodwill for whoever stood next to him.

And that was all that mattered. That song, that group. That and the anticipation of havoc after the match. Because it didn't matter who won. It never mattered who won. When it went way beyond what they could control, articles in the papers and documentaries asked questions like How Could This Happen? Bancher saw an interview with a lad whose face was gridded into little squares to disguise it, and his voice made to sound like Darth Vader. He told the interviewer how waiting for a match to end was like waiting for 'sex that you knew was goin' to happen. You jus' knew. That's the kind of excitement I'm talkin' about.' He talked about knives and broken bottles.

'As I said, Mr Bancher, we would very much like to… to liaise with you on the outcome of this matter.' The principal's head and shoulders came round the doorframe. Parting words. An injection of moral support. 'You need never feel alone in dealing with this.'

For a second, he fancies that she sees right into him. He thinks that he could tell her everything, every single thing leading up to this. How the carpet knife is all his fault. He could talk to her about the bad drop. She might feel sorry enough for him to take him out for a drink. She might even be fascinated by what he used to get up to, before his daughter was born. She might be one of those people interested in Badness as a Product of Social Deprivation. Likely she watched documentaries about crack babies and their parents.

She withdraws into her office. The door shuts with a thick wooden clap. Bancher stands in the school corridor, his heart going like a piston.

He levers himself away from the wall. Further down he hears running feet, the high spirits of a day's classes done. In the room off the principal's office, his daughter is waiting for him. He hasn't a clue what stern thing he could say to her. He's afraid she'll know how to look back at him.

Deaden the eyes.
Drop the lids.
Don't look at the lad in front of you.

Hen Night

David Butler

THE NOTE MUST HAVE BEEN STUCK to the underneath of her compact because it was precisely at the moment the reflected eye fixed her from out of its interior that the zigzag descent distracted her. It now sat perched at the edge of the washbasin, an innocuous butterfly dwarfed by her friend's cosmetics. Eleanor looked back at the iris sustained in the circular mirror and watched the mascara stick approach. But before the heavy stamen had engaged the lashes she pulled the stick away and looked again at the piece of paper.

It was small, no bigger than a cigarette skin, and looked to have been torn from a larger page. Yet someone had taken the trouble to fold it. She wondered when it had become stuck to her compact. Could it have been in her handbag? But she shook her head, looked once more at the eye in the mirror, hesitated over touching the lower lash with the brush. Her own dark pupil appeared to be examining her. Abruptly, Eleanor snapped the compact shut and replaced it into her bag. The mascara stick followed. Now she had been piqued by curiosity.

She looked again at the folded paper that teetered at the edge of the washbasin. How could it have been in her handbag? That made no sense. She glanced once at the door of the bathroom, listened to the hum of conversation that still overpowered the music in the next room. Then she snatched it up. Her hand acted now as though the origami insect might at any minute take flight. She opened it, smoothed out the folds, and allowed her eye run over the four short words scribbled along its interior. Too late, as though it had just stung her palm, she flung the note from her.

In the bathroom mirror a paralysed figure leaned towards her. A comic figure in bridal veil and Learner's plate. Her mouth was open, a perfect O. Her eyes, wide. But Eleanor was not looking at this woman. Eleanor was staring at where the note had fallen into the wash-hand basin. It lay on the soapy skin of water, face down, the words a line of dissolving shadow showing through wet paper. Four syllables, thirteen letters. Their force had struck her solar plexus so unexpectedly that she could not breathe.

It was a full minute before she regained enough composure to consider what she had read. Of course it was a joke, a sick joke, but which of her girlfriends could have been so malicious? Who would have acted in such bad taste? One corner of the paper had already dipped beneath the water's surface, the ink slowly dissolving into its warm undertow. Carefully, forensically, Eleanor lifted it out and laid it onto a white hand-towel. The ink had faded and spread like a lichen, but the trace remained legible. She looked again at the sentence, the thirteen letters, executed in a hand that was studiously casual.

I slept with Dan.

'We were beginning to think you were never coming out!' This was Chantal, Michelle's younger sister. Scarcely twenty, she was already tipsy. But Michelle, looking up at her from the sofa, addressed her with concern.

'Are you all right, El? You're very pale.'

The conversation in the room was sporadic now that the music had finished, and Eleanor felt that all eyes were watching her. She managed to raise a smile for their benefit.

'No, I'm fine. Really.'

'She's got cold feet!' Miriam—voluble, laughing Miriam. 'She's scared stiff so she is!' And the whole room was suddenly laughing. The bottles of wine were laughing, the CDs were laughing, the tortilla dips and the photographs and the potted plants were laughing, the poster by Matisse of the lovely odalisque, it too was laughing.

One of the girls attended to the music system and the speakers cackled back into life. Another, Katie, with red devil's horns and a tail, began to dance close and sexy with Michelle's huge teddy bear.

'Come on! You need to get one of these inside you.' A winking eye. 'Dutch courage!'

So that she took the glass that was being pressed into her hand and, touching the brim to her lip, she allowed the volatile spirit fill her lungs. Was it brandy? Eleanor glanced timidly around the faces that were admiring her, the eyes that were encouraging her. One pair among them must know of the somersault that had sacked her world. But then Michelle manoeuvred her out with one hand on the shoulder and another close about the waist and before they left the flat they began a dance that was even more provocative than Katie's.

How was it that she had got through the meal? The table, long and narrow, about which banter flew and jokes and ribald comments, the long table, with its closeness and deception and devious scrutiny. Four of the girls now had red devils' horns and Michelle, the white ears of a rabbit. A playboy bunny. Her own veil was a blur in the periphery of her vision.

I slept with Dan.

And she had no memory of having ordered or even having looked at the menu, so that when there was a mix-up first over the starters and then again over the main courses Miriam had laughed out 'Poor thing! She's so much in love, she's off her food so she is!'—*love* and *food* beaten flat by her Ulster accent. And Michelle, who was returning after a cigarette, had added from behind her: 'For once Miriam has a point. I've never seen you make such a poor effort at a marinara.' And then Katie had shouted 'Oh, my God, El, you never told us you were pregnant!' and the shrieks that followed disturbed the other tables so that the waiters frowned at their party.

Juvenile Chantal, giggling Chantal, was sitting diagonally opposite, and the Chianti had quite obviously gone to her head because as the desserts were arriving her flighty hand upset a wineglass. A huge stain spread over the cloth like a shadow, and a trickle dribbled onto Eleanor's thigh before she had a chance to move out of its path. 'Oh, my

God, I'm so sorry!' But Michelle, calm as a nurse, was able to apply a salt compress which lifted the worst of the crimson out of the silk.

Which of the eyes was watching with low malice?

It was late and the dance floor was far too crowded. A couple of foreign boys were busy entertaining two of the she-devils, but the rest of her group was ranged about a stand to the left of the bar. Drinks in various shapes and colours overpowered the miniature surface. But her girlfriends were tired of being jostled, and the mood was subdued.

I slept with Dan.

Each time it returned with the force of a blow.

Then at some point Michelle had taken her by the arm and steered her across the dance floor in the direction of the rest rooms. *What in God's name do you pair get up to in there together? The sorority of the toilet!* That was Dan all over, the crow's feet and the squinting eyes. He was forever goading Michelle. He got on so well with all of her girlfriends. Only her brother had never warmed to his easy manner. So was it possible… No! No! Eleanor could not let her imagination go there. She shut her eyes and drove down the sudden rebellion in her entrails. Not Dan.

And, after they had queued, the dank, buttocky closeness of the bathroom, so heavy with sprays, made her feel faint. The truth is she was not used to drink. Like a true friend Michelle had seen that the others had not pressed too many spirits on her, but there was only so much that one could do. This was meant to be Eleanor's night.

'Talk to me, El. What is it? You haven't been yourself all evening.'

Michelle was standing at the wash-basin beside her. As she waited for Eleanor to reply she began to touch up her lips, kissing a tissue paper and then pouting provocatively at her reflection. She was very attractive, Michelle, when she made the effort.

'I don't know. I…'

And suddenly she was sobbing. Great gobs of anxiety swelled up from her guts and poured out of her mouth. She teetered, gripped the wash-basin. She felt her friend's arms steady her. 'For God's sake, what is it? Ellie!' But throat and lungs were racked with spasms and she could not speak. She opened her mouth, and no air came from her lungs. No word could pass through the stricture in her throat. It was as if terror had seized her.

Outside. It is almost three o'clock.

'Can you talk?'

'...'

'I'm sorry, you're breaking up on me.'

'...'

'No. Listen. Will you ring me back?'

There is too much bustle and noise on the streets, and the connection is fragile. Brittle. The girl in the white rabbit ears glances quickly at the anonymous faces that grin past. Then she looks instead to the squat phone that nests in her palm. Even outside, even at this late hour, she is reluctant to raise her voice. Perhaps the walls will overhear.

She lights a cigarette and glances back towards the bouncer. As she exhales blue smoke into the night air she thinks over the evening's vicissitudes. She thinks of the moment that her best friend disappeared into her bathroom before they left the flat. All the while Eleanor was in there, a rage of butterflies had troubled her stomach.

She draws again on the cigarette and squints in the direction of the club. She does not want to think about what she has done. She does not want to think. Her eyes deflect to the phone. What words will she say to him? How will she have the nerve to tell him?

She flicks away the cigarette, half-smoked. Inside her, the rage of butterflies is relentless. She glances hurriedly at the entrance to the club. But if Eleanor were to step out, now, this minute? Could she admit? Beg her forgiveness? Go back?

A vibration shocks her hand. A light tenses, dilates, bickers.

She raises the phone and reads, in panic, in relief, his flashing name.

The Dead Hotel

Kevin Power

June 11th

THERE ARE NO FLIGHTS LANDING ON THE ISLAND ANYMORE. Ours was the very last one. At Palma—gingerly, ears ravaged by the faulty air-pressure of an economy flight from Dublin—we hauled our bags off the lethal treadmill and staggered out into the sunshine. Didn't get lost once. You couldn't miss the Arrivals Hall; there were no other tourists in it. Just the clerks and the baggage-handlers, clerking and handling baggage.

On holiday in Mallorca. Isabel, Chris, Eimear, and my good self. White rented rooms, sapphire heft of a lilting pool. Female flesh set quivering by my playful slap as I walk past Isabel, who is draped across a poolside plastic lounger as I write this, reading an airport paperback called *Sex Lives of the Nazi Doctors*.

Our block is called Palm Tree Villas. There is one withered palm tree, and a pudgy fair-haired boy who stands beside it. He's about nine years old. That's what he does: he stands beside the tree, from noon to midnight. I've seen him there every day so far. That first afternoon, as we shuffled past on our way to the apartment, I spotted a fat, brown three-inch cockroach squatting on the bark of the tree. The fair-haired boy was watching it—scrutinising it, really, like a doctor worrying over a stool sample—and as I came level with him he reached out a hand and closed a sweaty, patient fist over the twitching segments of the insect's body. I don't know what he did with it.

Today is my first sober day. I got out of bed early, at noon, and I had all sorts of holiday plans... but it's late afternoon now, and you don't want to go outside in that murderous heat. It punches you in the gut every time you step outside. The gut, the face, the shoulder blades.

But the holiday is doing us good. I can see it in Isabel, of course, but in Chris and Eimear most of all. Their drinking has improved. I take this to be a good sign. They've stayed in bed with hangovers all day, which means I am alone with Isabel. So. Things are looking up.

June 12th

This morning Isabel and I went to the supermarket. She was wearing ragged cotton shorts, and if I let myself fall a few paces behind I could take in the peerless sway of her ass as she walked through the shade under the awnings. We stocked up on beer and whiskey. 'You'll dehydrate yourselves,' Chris said as, lounging on the terrace, we punctured our first cans of the day. But I already feel comprehensively dehydrated. I feel like a husk, laid out to dry beneath the stinging sun. I'm not quite drunk as I write this; a few more rum-and-cokes will take me nicely towards bedtime, and for those I'll have to head to the bar in Paradise Isle, the neighbouring apartment block. There's a barbecue on there this evening. Americans and Brits in Hawaiian shirts are already assembling by the clear pool, counting the roaches and mosquitoes that flap against its surface tension.

The fair-haired boy was there again today, keeping his perpetual vigil beside his wilting tree. Still no sign of his parents.

June 13th

Isabel and I skulked by the edge of the pool as Chris and Eimear waited for food at the barbecue. Some of the Americans had found a haunch of beef for sale at the supermarket, and were doling out chunks of it from beside the grill like bourgeois businessmen at a charity drive. I was watching Chris, who was in shallow conversation with a loud-shirted American.

Eimear arrived, carrying drooping paper plates of bloody meat. 'I don't know how cooked it is,' she said, ' I don't even know *what* it is. But it beats having to cook for ourselves.'

I didn't touch any of the beef. Alcohol used to sharpen my appetite, but now it seems to do the opposite: my appetite is crushed, blunted, pulped. Yesterday I picked up the book that Isabel totes around and read that Dr. Mengele liked to sodomise young Jewish maidens before ordering that they be flayed alive. I think I saw a film about this once.

Chris brought his American friend over. 'This is Jerry,' he said. 'He's from Australia. From *Cranberry*, Australia.'

Jerry grinned, as though this were a terrific joke.

'Oh,' Isabel squealed, 'I lived in Canberra for three months!'

'*Cranberry*,' Chris insisted.

We stood around, holding our drinks. Jerry studied Isabel with creased, alarming eyes. I put my arm around her freckled shoulders.

Jerry leaned into us. 'Have you guys heard the rumours?'

I smiled a Buddhist's smile: sharer of knowledge, hoarder of inner peace.

'No,' Isabel said, wriggling out from under my arm. 'What's the story now?'

Jerry gave a professional's grimace. 'Someone was telling me the other day that for five minutes CNN was reporting strikes over the DRC. They killed the story, though, right after. You know, cos they didn't want anyone to know about it. Like the massacres in Tennessee.'

'We still don't know,' I said loftily, 'what actually happened—'

'And what would that mean?' Isabel asked.

'Fallout,' Jerry the Australian said. 'Just fallout. Here, there, and everywhere.'

My memories of the rest of the night are confused. I can tell you what I saw, or what I think I saw: Isabel talking to Jerry, Jerry talking to Eimear (he's talking about birth defects: how reports of them are spreading from somewhere to somewhere else), Chris bellowing *Cranberry!* at anyone who'll listen, Isabel and Jerry disappearing somewhere, the gasps of amusement and fear as a helicopter makes a flyby overhead; an American screaming that he's burned his hand on the barbecue; Chris telling me he's discovered something important but he's not sure what; the blackened, furry remains of the side of beef being thrown into the pool, turning the water a misty charcoal grey; me, searching for Isabel, but there is no Isabel to be found. I don't even remember finding my way back to our apartment. I folded into my own bed, though, and I lay there, eyes riveted on the ceiling, listening to the angry sounds of the barbecue as they faded with the first light of another burning day.

From the balcony this morning—crinkled newspaper in one hand, sprightly orange juice in the other—I saw the fat blonde boy move for the very first time. He abandoned his tree and went to look at the ruined pool, fixing his equable gaze on the black corpse of beef under the water. 'Hooray,' I said, 'it's alive.' But there was no one around to hear me.

With this morning's hangover came the sad slow-burn of remorseful jealousy. Of course Isabel had fucked Jerry. Every morning now, more people wake up in the wrong room. I decided that if I found Jerry, I would kill him.

Chris shuffled onto the balcony and winced down at the remains of the pool. '*That* was a good one.'

'I don't remember it.'

'Neither do I. I'm going on the physical evidence.' He took from his pocket a little black notebook, and began to scribble something.

Inside my gut a miniature Chernobyl, a toy town Three Mile Island, fizzed and crackled. Chris closed his notebook. 'Shall we begin the hunt?'

'The hunt?'

'For Eimear. She's out there somewhere.'

'Why? Where?'

'She went off with the Cranberry Man. Made me promise to track her down this morning, if she didn't find her way home.'

'Where's Isabel?' I croaked.

'In bed,' Chris said. 'Better bring her some juice.'

Two hours later we found Eimear in an empty apartment, identical to ours but with a smashed television, and with an investigative line of ants powdered across the kitchen lino. Eimear didn't wake up, so we carried her home. The room we found her in had *drugs*. You know what I mean? It had *drugs* like other rooms have carpet or furniture. But there was no sign of Jerry, our man from Canberra, and no food in the fridge, no clothes in the wardrobe.

June 16th

They still haven't cleaned the water. Now you can't swim (nobody dares to go near the ocean), and you can't sit by the pool: its restful shimmer has been replaced by a static grey slime. Parties have moved inside. You can hear them, faintly, at the peak of noon, during the worst of the heat. This evening I went for a walk along the beach. The sand was full of insects, white skittish things that scattered along in your footsteps. I ran into Jerry. We went for a drink at one of the beachside bars. Of course I had no reason to kill him now. The bar was one of those ex-pat places, run by a middle-aged British couple. Pinned on the walls was a lifetime's worth of football memorabilia (remember football? It seems laughable, now, all that organisation). Jerry talked at length about the political predicament. Some friends of his arrived: a hippy girl with tie-dyed shirt and braided hair, and another young Australian named Alex, who told us he was on his way home from Morocco but was stranded now, marooned. 'It's Eden here,' Jerry told him. 'Paradise, mate.' We ordered more Sangria.

We headed back to the apartments, but as soon as you leave the little seafront the streets are empty, voices rebound from the whitewashed walls. Turn a corner and there they are: a dozen men in black military gear, gas masks slung casually around their thick necks, building a roadblock. Jerry, Hawaiian shirt open at the collar, palms raised in a placatory advance, shouted something in pidgin Spanish. 'It's alright,' he said over his shoulder, 'they're just setting up a checkpoint.' He went towards one of the soldiers, who greeted him by gently slinging the butt of his rifle into Jerry's stomach. A skilful, pinched chop to the back of the neck sent Jerry all the way down. The lead soldier motioned to two others—it was a lazy wave, a valediction almost—who came over and kicked Jerry until he stopped moving.

The lead soldier stared at us for a minute. Then he smiled cheerfully, like a prosperous *maitre d'*, and waved us on.

After a while we wound up in a dead-end street. Dry sheets flapped below washing lines, short steps led to barred doors. The girl sat down beneath some railings and began to cry: she was pregnant, and Jerry was the father, and now what would she do? I embraced her. It seemed to be what she wanted. When I looked up, Alex had gone. When I tried to stand I braced my palm on a shard of glass. Blood welled, generously. I used a fragment of my T-shirt to bandage it.

When I got back to our apartment Isabel and Chris were cooking dinner, and Eimear was curled in a chair on the balcony, smoking and turning the pages of a newspaper. They were busily happy. Chris noticed my wounded hand. And the boy was there, again, today. What does he know about us, about me? What's his game?

June 17th

Last night Isabel and I slept in the same bed. I pressed my bandaged palm to her flesh where her T-shirt rose a little. I dreamed of a bristling Irish woodland, after rain. Broken branch and rustling twig, a microscopic ecology of glinting rain and shaken leaves. The sky opens itself above me. Someone is out here, heart beating too quickly—not from a chase but from something else, a sense of otherness. Guilt or ghost or apprehension.

June 19th

Chris has shut himself in his room with his notebook and the newspapers. He speaks to us through the door. He asked me to get him more tabloids, more broadsheets. I went to the supermarket, where the shelves are emptying. The corridors of Palm Tree Villas are filling with rubbish. This morning I found three suitcases in the third floor stairwell, bulging with clothes and ready to go. But nobody arrived to claim them, and they were still there this evening, as the parties kicked into gear.

June 22nd

The fat boy. His clothes change. This much I do know. He wears a different T-shirt every day. There is always a white shield of lotion on his nose. And what does he do? He guards the palm tree. This palm tree seems to need guarding, too. It needs him to look after it. He touches it occasionally, reaching out a raw hand. He takes away the swarming cockroaches. I watch him, from the willowy shade of the poolside showers. He gently lifts away the querulous roaches and… I know what he does with them now.

June 23rd

Chris has not emerged. He has a theory, Eimear insists, about why all this is going on. 'It has to do with the durability of tourism,' he tells her through the door. 'It's essentially an amoral activity. Calamity has no effect on its processes.' Isabel and I lie awake at night, listening to the punctured cascade of broken glass as windows break all over the complex. I can feel a sort of toxic swell, flowing outwards from the wound in my hand. I shouldn't have cut it, in retrospect. That was a bad move.

Isabel and Eimear sent me down for more drinks. In the Palm Tree Villas bar half a dozen Englishmen were aimlessly perambulating. When they'd calmed me down (I must have been shouting) they told me that the bar appeared to have run out of alcohol. I went back upstairs and told the crew.

'How could they have allowed this to happen?' Isabel asked through her tears. At the sink I unwound the bandage from my injured hand. I may have just imagined a greenish tinge to the edges of the folded cut.

I was woken at five in the morning by what sounded like a gaggle of kids trouping past my window on their way to school. I stumbled to the balcony and looked out over the blackened swimming pool towards the edges of the complex. Down the little seafront street they came, a hundred of them or more, tourists in their shorts and sunglasses, carrying rucksacks and suitcases, clutching bundles of clothes and bottles of vodka like refugee mothers fleeing a war zone. No one appeared to be hurrying. Isabel joined me at the crumbling parapet. 'Where are they coming from?' she asked. I could hardly see her in the dawn light. 'From the hotel,' I said. Some of the women were carrying televisions and trouser presses, and the men brought with them cordless hairdryers and shower caps. As the dawn began to subtly burn, the march continued, young men and women with varying degrees of suntan pressing their sneakers and flip-flops to the concrete road. I watched them until the sun came up and the last of them had disappeared into the town. Isabel went back to bed, squeezing my hand as she left. I barely noticed the human warmth of her fingers. I can't say why, but I was fascinated—even mesmerised—by the stately progress of the hotel guests. I knew there was no reason for it. Even if I had seen military men, densely powerful in their uniforms, shepherding (gentle word) the walking masses, I would have known. There was no reason for it. Throughout it all, the fat boy stood stoically by his palm tree, unstirred by the spectacle of abandonment taking place a hundred yards away. I watched until the last of their cushioned feet had drifted out of earshot, and I was left alone with the contents of my own astonished heart.

Then I went inside and drained the last mercurial shimmer from Eimear's bottle of vodka.

June 26th

The hotel looms above us now. Chris believes something serious happened there, and that whatever it was will soon happen to Palm Tree Villas. Eimear has collected all of our bottles and emptied their listless dregs into a single tumbler, from which we are allowed to take hourly sips; but it isn't working. I'm sobering up. The cut in my hand has taken to bleeding peaceably during the night. This is no longer the holiday I envisioned.

Chris has begun to pass notes underneath his door. One read: *This is all we have left: the poetry of sun and shadow on a fuselage, the poetry of airports and coach travel, the poetry of unnoticed electrical sockets and wipe-clean floors.* Another read: *Can't we all just get along?*

Eimear stares at them for hours, attempting to make sense of them. The boy the boy the boy the boy the boy

June 29th

Last night, at around midnight, my fever broke. While everyone else slept I cleaned out the cut on my hand. I checked out the dawn. I looked over my notes here. I don't remember a lot of this stuff, or why it seemed important—the exodus from the hotel, the soldiers, Chris's notes. What is important—what deserves my immediate and full attention—is the fact that *we have totally run out of beer.*

To kill time I left the apartment and wandered round the complex. Several rooms had been taken over by feral cats, little walking bags of tetanus and fever. Two floors above us a party seemed to be in progress. The lifts were broken, so I risked the stairwells: two unconscious girls in football jerseys, but nothing to be afraid of. The penthouse door had been taken off its hinges. I went inside, kicking my way through crumpled cans and spinning bottles. Three girls and a guy were basking in the balcony hot tub. The guy was Jerry, tenderly cradling a bottle of Jack Daniels and squinting at me through two poppy-coloured black eyes.

'Howdy, mate,' he said guardedly.

'Jerry,' I said. 'I'm looking for beer. Have you seen any?'

There was a silence.

'No,' Jerry said. 'Not here, mate.'

When I got back to our apartment the fair-haired boy was standing on our balcony, staring down at the motionless swimming pool.

We gathered around Chris's locked door and confronted the reality of our situation. What we decided was this: Isabel and I will take the fair-haired boy and go to the empty hotel, to check for supplies of food and drink. The idea was Chris's. He is curious about what happened at the hotel. We'll set out at nightfall, when things are quiet, when the screams from Paradise Isle have dwindled into restless silence and the troops by the seashore have gone home for the night.

June 30th

We set out along the beach, at the edge of the incoming tide. The hotel had its own section of beach, marked off by a cluster of baking rocks. The building still had electricity: yellow light flickered in some windows, and the open-air bar—the only way into the hotel from the beach—still cranked hilarious holiday tunes into the summer twilight. We picked our way among the tables. The boy led us through the bar, with its rolling tables and spilled drinks, into the main lobby.

'It's deserted,' Isabel said. And deserted it was. The revolving door had partly shattered: spidery contortions of seminal white threaded their way through the sheets of glass. Clothes, condoms, and books were scattered on the plush floor and across the leather couches. Behind the mahogany reception desk the keys still hung in their numbered slots. Newspapers waved with the breeze from the air conditioning. Most striking of all, the cash registers had been overturned. An eruption of paper money and credit card receipts covered the floor behind the desk. There was blood and beaded glass in the pile of the carpet. And there was *silence*: tombal, meditative silence, silence that does not expect to be disturbed.

The fair-haired boy went straight through the devastated lobby to the alcove where they kept the elevators, and pressed the call-button.

Isabel kicked at a crumpled, bloody T-shirt. 'What do you think happened?'

'They cleared out,' I said stupidly. I looked around, turned a complete circle, but there was nothing, and nobody, just the invasive stillness of evening on the island, that time when all the kids come out to play.

A feathery *ping*, like a microwave's cue, announced the arrival of a lift. The boy's excitement caught our attention. We followed him into one of the glacial, mirrored cages, and he pressed, without giving it much thought, the button for the fifty-fifth floor. Isabel and I glumly preened our reflections in the golden wall.

I wasn't surprised, of course, when the doors opened into total darkness. But Isabel was. '*Shit,*' she said. Even the fat boy seemed to hesitate a little. He scratched a blistered ear with his pudgy fingers. We stared into the black corridor. It reminded me of a dream I had once, as a child, with a child's unreasonable fear of unlit spaces. *Monsters*, I thought, *we'll find monsters in the dark.* But the boy led us inevitably forward into the corridor, and turned left, into a patch of cool air. It was even quieter up here: the bristling, ogre's silence of a large hotel. I took Isabel's hand and we followed the boy.

It was a strangely peaceful pursuit. We could have been calmly stumbling for a quarter of an hour. Eventually we hit a cold wall, the end of the corridor. Off to our right, a tongue of amber light lolled across the carpet. The boy stood at the door of an open room, looking at something inside. I walked towards him. Did Isabel come with me? She must have. We were alone now, waiting for our monsters. The boy disappeared inside his room.

It was an ordinary hotel room, odourless and without character. The only thing you noticed was the TV, squatting in the corner. Ghostly programmes trickled through the intermittent static. It seemed to be a news report: you could see roadblocks, piles of dead Americans, freeze-frame shots of a grey explosion. The fair-haired boy watched it with touristic awe. Isabel went to the window and looked through the curtains, out at the fires that erupted beyond the bay.

I stood behind her, and somehow—you know how these things work out—I put my arms around her little waist, and she arched her back welcomingly. When she turned to kiss me I wasn't surprised. I fitted the cup of my injured hand to her breast (all the time tuned in to the permanent crash and buzz of the TV news) and we kissed more earnestly. We began to climb out of our clothes. The fair-haired boy watched television while we fucked on the edge of the hotel bed. Around us the hotel did not wake. We were very quiet, Isabel and I, and afterwards we cried as undramatically as we could.

When we had finished I noticed that the fat boy was holding a box of matches that bore the logo of the hotel bar. He offered them to me without emphasis. I took them and set a fire in the corner of the room, at the feet of the drawn curtains.

We left the boy watching television in the room on the fifty-fifth floor and found our way back to the lobby, and then to the beach. Still naked, we ran off along the temperate sand, feeling sick and filthy, desperate to find our way home.

July 1st

Mum rang today to tell me that I passed my exams and that my enrolment papers for next year are in the post. Our flight home, she reminded me (as if I were still a kid) was in three days. 'Dad and I missed you,' she said. She was even starting to cry, a bit. I have to move out next year. There's only so much of his parents a man can be expected to take.

A Week of Little Deaths

Martin Malone

LATE EVENING AT HEUSTON STATION I check the digital timetable, relieved to see that I've made it in plenty of time for the last train home. I buy a paper mug of coffee in a café adjoining the station's pub, weak coffee, strong price. I think about doing an Eddie Hobbs but the guy serving doesn't look as though he could handle my grief. You'd think by his puss that his customers were ripping him off.

I think about Dad, lying in a hospital bed not ten-minutes walk from the station. Rarely, I suppose, does anyone ever stop to think about never hearing his father's voice again. Normally it doesn't steal upon you till your father's dead and the missing then is a whole missing, not a partial one.

There is a dull grey and cold light in the almost empty station, as though the residue of night has drifted in. The air is tainted with smells of river sewage and diesel oil, of dampness. And a strange energy thrives; of a million or more comings and goings for a million and one different reasons.

Across from me sit a woman and a man. She wants to be heard talking about her book, while the man is uncomfortable with such self-aggrandisement. The flea in his ear shows in the shift of his arse, and the way his hand comes to his mouth—trapping a *please shut the fuck up talking about yourself.*

I don't bother to finish my coffee.

I walk along platform 8 and pick a carriage with a scattering of passengers and sit in a window seat, intertwine my fingers on the blue topped table. A notice under the window rim says the paint spraying was done by an award-winning Irish company.

I own a lingering summer cold which I blame on the changeable weather; wear a jacket and you're too warm, don't and you feel the cold. I've been to see the old man in hospital. A week ago he'd undergone twelve hours of surgery to remove a tumour from his throat. His voice will return but it won't have the same quality, the surgeon has said. He will also be restricted in the type of foods he can eat. Skin grafts will follow. This is all in the future, that fluid and indefinite entity people try to make definite.

It had been heartening though to hear the surgeon speak so positively—but then he paused, his face changing expression before he issued a note of caution. Of course there would be tests to see if they'd contained the cancer; that it hadn't spread.

From a man who had learned the hard way not to be definite.

My mother said he'd gotten the cancer in the right place, which made me ask myself what fucking planet she was on. She'd meant, of course, that he'd gotten it in a part of the body where the cure rate was a high percentage.

She comes out with a lot of stuff like that—things you could pick several meanings to. Bugs me sometimes the way she says things. The old man on the other hand was never a great one to talk unless fortified with drink, then he found himself believing he had a wisdom the world and its son simply had to hear. To his credit, drunk or sober he was never ambiguous.

When the train pulls out, it is, I think, a slow going into the darkness. The city lights are left behind, the night and my own image stare at me from the window glass. A ghostly reflection. I am in my father's likeness—a thought shrill and sharp enough to have me search my cheeks and throat.

By the time I reach Kildare forty minutes later, it's drizzling. I climb the wet concrete steps and cross the railway bridge, its studded steel floor vibrating under the pitter-patter of feet and roll of suitcase wheel.

I'd parked my car in the station car park, an old beat-up Ford Fiesta whose engine cracked a week after I'd bought it in a garage, that my father said, would cheat a blind man out of his change.

'A bit late for the learning', I'd said to him.

'You never ask, you never tell me anything—like that shitty tattoo you got done—you came over and asked me what I thought of it—you didn't ask me my opinion before you went and got it—the car is the same old story.'

The old man was right. I have a habit of asking him for his advice when it's far too late for the asking. A masochist thing with me, I think—wanting to hear I told you so.

I live in an apartment close to the station. A Spanish-villa type apartment block that within five years has acquired a cheated look; born in the wrong country, the weather too hard for its bones. The swamp it was built on shows up in green patches on its façade. A plethora of *For Sale* signs thumb from behind low walls.

My father was involved in soccer. He won junior and senior amateur international caps, and had been a day away from signing professional terms with Aston Villa when he broke his leg playing against Shamrock Rovers. He lost a yard of pace and a further yard of nerve—never the same player.

He used to go to all the international senior matches and roar his head off. Germany 1990 was our pilgrimage year. Jack Charlton played his kind of tactical game. Chris Hughton and Ray Houghton who put the ball in the English net signed my T-shirt. I was nine back then and the day we were to leave for Stuttgart I didn't want to travel and he'd to talk me into it. His breath smelled of mint and when he asked me why I didn't want to go with him I said I'd seen the Nazis on TV and Hitler and all, and that Mam said the English fans would hop the shite out of us. He looked hard at Mam and shook his head. Then he said he wouldn't let anything bad happen to me.

In my apartment I put the keys on the granite countertop and ring Mam. After the call I take consolation in the fact that she is the same towards my father's friends, ringing those who have not visited him and others whose visits haven't been as prolific as she believes they ought to be. She does not understand that some people are uncomfortable about hospitals and find it difficult to speak to someone as seriously ill as Dad. In addition some of those she's called moved out of Dad's social circle a long time ago and would have resented the past catching up with them.

If I had a brother, a sister, things might be different. Sometimes I feel it is all too much, my mother too much, and think about getting away from the town, not having a fixed notion of where I might go. Knowing it is the notion of leaving that gives me solace but the actuality of it would reef my heart, for I love the town and if I am unsure of my love for my mother I have no such doubt regarding my love for my father. Also there is Heather.

Because our relationship is in its embryonic stage I do not involve her in the family's crisis, other than to give her brief daily reports which I amn't too sure she wants to receive. Hospital bulletin, I joke, trying to read a blank face. She has a habit of feeling a tendril of her long black hair, like she is forever contemplating matters. Occasionally, I sense her attention drift from me whenever we are out, but before it grows to a slight, an act of ignorance, she's back all smiles, bubbling, focused again, aborting my rising umbrage.

I do not make the hospital the next day, nor the day after. I tell Mam when she calls that my head cold isn't getting any better and I don't want to risk passing my germs on to the patients. I sneeze on cue, which is a coincidence and not contrived.

I'm feeling a little down in myself. I did not visit Dad because Miss Blankface had said I was rushing her. She suggested that we take a step backwards and asked me not to contact her for a few days. Staggering news, delivered as she toyed with her hair. It hurt me, for I am not stupid. If Dad sees me in this mood he will think I've heard bad news about him. I will have to tell him the truth. And though he cannot speak I'd hate to see *I told you so* register in his eyes.

I am alone with Dad. Mam has gone to get something to eat in a café. She did not say this in front of Dad, who can't eat solids and probably won't for a long time to come.

He lies there, on his back, throat bandaged, drip tube in his forearm. Drowsy. He writes hello on a writing pad and I think of when I was away in the States for six months and how Mam wrote and Dad didn't. Now I understand why as I read his childish scrawl in a spiral-bound notebook. Dad's thin fingers look out of place holding the pen. After a couple of minutes he drops the pen and looks to the ceiling for guidance.

I say, 'Mam, she's doing your head in?'

Dad nods an almost imperceptible nod.

'Mine too.'

He goes to pick up the pen but I say, 'Yeah, she means well, I know, Dad.'

His finger and thumb relax.

I sit for a long while talking to Dad, answering his own questions for him, he nodding in agreement, once smiling the ghost of a smile.

The years have brought us to this—a woman panicking at the notion of living a life without her husband, a son not knowing where his place is but trying to find it all the same.

It has been a week of little deaths: Heather adjourning our relationship so she could date an ex-boyfriend who's back in town from the States, the death of my father's voice—for now a nod, a scratch of pen, in the future it'll be a resurrected mutation of a voice, a strangled sort of cry—and even that much isn't definite.

Red Truck

Maria Behan

'WHERE ARE WE? THE ARMAGH TURN-OFF 'S MILES BACK,' Fintan said, eyeing the fields and farmhouses he hadn't noticed for the past ten minutes. 'This isn't the way to the planetarium.'

'We're not going there,' Sylvia said. Her voice was as hard as her square jaw, which she worked from side to side like she was settling a plug of tobacco.

'We talked about it all week. Why aren't we going to the planetarium?'

'Because you've got something else to do,' she replied.

'What do you mean?' Fintan asked, but Sylvia didn't answer.

Fintan was a month shy of his fiftieth birthday. Others had begun to use the pile-up of years against him, advising him to act his age, get a real job, save for retirement. But Fintan couldn't imagine needing a pension. In fact, he was surprised to be reaching fifty. Not because of a romantic notion of dying young, it was just that he hadn't counted on time working the way it did. Somehow he'd thought that the years would progress slowly until he decided exactly what to do with them. Instead they had built up stealthily, relentlessly, like dust.

His time problem was compounded by the fact that the markers had become indistinct since his schooling ended nearly three decades before. There were occasional exhibitions of his sculptures, which had no clear trajectory of either improvement or deterioration; and a shifting cast of girlfriends, which did display a downward spiral of late. His partners were always the same age—their late 20s—but in recent years they were factory seconds of young womanhood, not the pristine article. Sylvia, with her headmistress's demeanour and flabby stomach, was a case in point. She was an art student. They were always art students.

As they approached the next turn, the penny dropped.

'Drive on, damn it,' Fintan said as the car slowed to enter a lane that wound through an apple orchard. 'There's no way I'm going there.'

'You have to,' Sylvia said. 'The house is sold, your poor mother's moving to her sister's next week, and you still haven't cleared your things out of the attic. Your brothers did that months ago.'

'Why are you involved? You're not part of the family.'

'Your mother rang a few days ago and asked me to urge you to come over here and cart off your stuff. Her phrase was 'Use whatever influence you have.' Do you think she was insinuating something sexual?'

'My mother never insinuates anything sexual,' Fintan said, turning away from Sylvia to look out the window. 'So you tricked me,' he added quietly.

She parked the car in front of a large brick house with four gables and two pillars, a vision of Protestant prosperity though it had been built by his father, a Catholic who was as good a chameleon as he was a businessman.

'I'm sorry, Fintan,' Sylvia said with a sigh and an apologetic smile he found unconvincing. 'Just get it done, and I'll pick you up in two hours.'

Fintan shot her a glare, a skill he excelled at since his left eye had developed a squint. Sylvia ignored him, feigning interest in her chipped silver nail polish. He finally gave up and left the car with a snort.

The front yard was overgrown, but otherwise the scene was familiar. The lawn and house were surrounded by apple trees, pruned into umbrella shapes for easy picking. It was May, and the trees' pink-and-white blossoms reminded Fintan of the dewy flesh of Rubens' cherubs. Scores of bumblebees thrummed through the air, some so heavy with pollen they had trouble gaining altitude.

In a week or so, the flowers would start falling off the trees. 'When the petal drops, sex stops,' Fintan recalled his father observing in previous springtimes. He had always smiled wistfully while saying it, though Fintan found the notion chilling. Maybe for you, old man, but not for me, he'd thought.

The air outside held the same ancient sweetness as every May, but the smell was different inside the house. Since his father's death, the leaden odour of meat had dissipated. He'd insisted on a fry every morning, followed by a dinner of beef, lamb or, in a pinch, pork. Fintan's mother had faithfully served her husband the flesh that would eventually kill him, though she herself was 'almost a vegetarian'— which she admitted with a mischievous titter, as if confessing to something racy.

Fintan went towards the kitchen, envisioning his mother in her mid-morning occupations of ironing and listening to a radio call-in programme. Her gentle tut-tuts over the antics of Sinead O'Connor or Ian Paisley would be mimicked by Joey the cockatiel, whose shrill cries made him seem the more incensed of the two. But when Fintan opened the kitchen door, his mother was nowhere in sight and Joey's cage was shrouded in a green plaid cloth. Fearing the worst, Fintan lifted the cover, but Joey was merely asleep on his perch. His yellow crest, which usually bristled straight up from his head, was tilted to the side, making him look slovenly, or drunk.

There was nothing for Fintan to do but go up to the attic. He pulled open the trap door, unfolded the rickety ladder, and carefully mounted the rungs. When he reached the top, he smelled the slow rot of expensive cloth and saw thousands of dust motes dancing in the sunlight, making the air seem alive but unhealthy.

As Sylvia had said, the attic had been largely cleaned out, but there were still a few trunks and about a half-dozen boxes. He began rummaging through the ones marked 'Finn.' Most of the items he found were eminently discardable: a desiccated turkey foot, school notebooks crammed with vicious caricatures of teachers now retired or dead, a clutch of handball medals and a first-prize essay certificate—two of the areas he'd excelled in as a child that did him no good as an adult.

When he pulled a dinky truck from the second-to-last box, he gave a low whistle. Its fake chrome accents were nearly chipped off, but the red metal body retained a fierce gleam. Fingering the toy's rust-soldered wheels, Fintan was transported back to his sixth birthday.

It had been his favourite gift, a thing of unblemished newness that shone out from the steaming heap of his older brothers' cast-offs. Shane, the eldest, was a bully of the old school, though by that time he'd turned thirteen and rarely expended his energy on short-pantsers like Fintan. Unfortunately, that wasn't the case with the next in line. Peter was big enough to overpower and humiliate Fintan, but not mature enough to disdain wasting his strength on a scrawny fledgling.

Untainted by his brothers' foul juices, the truck seemed to hint at the possibility of manliness and eventual escape from the humiliations heaped on him by Shane and Peter. Fintan ignored his other presents that day—an Aran jumper and an illustrated children's Bible—to play with the truck down in the orchard. His father had three lorries for his apple business, so Fintan was acquainted with the perils of haulage. He constructed scenarios involving lost loads, dodgy weigh bridges and dishonest freight inspectors. His father, who had skipped the birthday party to cut down some storm-damaged trees, overheard his theatrics.

'You'll join the business one day, so you will,' he said, ruffling Fintan's dirty hair until it stood up like reeds.

A month later, the truck remained the first thing Fintan thought of when he woke up. But it wasn't parked in its usual spot on his bedside table that June morning. Indeed, it was nowhere in his room, or the kitchen, or the parlour, or the bath. After he'd searched the entire house twice, a hideous certainty descended on him: one of his brothers had taken the toy out of spite. Over the years, they had bloodied his nose, pulled down his pants, and squeezed the sides of his lips while forcing him to repeat, 'I'm a pretty baby' again and again. But the pilfering of his truck was too much to bear.

Fintan went into the kitchen and threw the only tantrum of his life. While his mother and brothers looked on, he shrieked, stamped, broke a dish and went stiff as a corpse, then repeated the routine with minor embellishments. He took an apple from the wooden bowl on the table, took a big bite, and spat it at his brothers, hitting Shane on the neck. He held his breath until he crumpled to the floor.

His mother ran to get her husband from the orchard. He slammed open the door, rushed over to his red-faced son—who was writhing on the floor like a seizure victim at that stage—and picked him up by the ankles. Fintan was almost relieved by this intervention, since he hadn't a clue how to end his performance. Looking at his frightened mother and suspicion-tainted brothers from his upside-down vantage point, he felt defeated yet righteous. He quieted down, his father scolded him gently before going back to work, and no one mentioned the toy truck again.

At the end of the summer, Fintan's mother asked him to carry some lunch up to the men stacking bales in the top cornfield. It was a sweltering day, so she draped a white handkerchief over his head to protect him from the sun. On his way back from delivering the flasks of tea and melting blackberry jam sandwiches, Fintan noticed something lying in the stubble: his lorry. It was dirty and its tyres had lost their smell of rubbery goodness, but it was undoubtedly his red truck.

Confronted with the evidence, his memory suddenly yielded an image. A few months back, he'd been playing with the truck by the edge of the field when he was startled by the sound of Peter roaring his name. The summons might have meant anything from 'Mam wants you for dinner' to 'prepare for a beating,' so Fintan decided to dive into the field and hide among the green stalks. The truck must have fallen out of his pocket.

Joy gave way to despair when he realised he couldn't possibly admit that his accusation against his brothers had been unfounded. He took the handkerchief from his head, wrapped the truck in it, and sat under a tree with the bundle in his lap to consider his options. He could throw the toy in the river so it could never implicate him—and, more important, absolve his brothers. But that was too final. He could give it away to one of his schoolmates, but that was too altruistic. He finally decided to defer his decision and hide the lorry in the false bottom of his wardrobe.

There it lay over the years, the first bit of contraband in a cache that would eventually include the word 'nude' written in wavering cursive on the back of an envelope, a few catalogues that he'd pilfered from his mother (the pages always fell open to the lingerie sections), a *Playboy* his cousin had mailed him from America after much begging and bribing, and a small chunk of hash. The last time Fintan had seen the truck was when he'd moved out for good after college. He had cleared out his hiding space, taking the gear and the *Playboy*, but leaving the catalogues and the lorry behind in a box marked 'Finn's Miscellany.'

Fintan uttered a feeble 'vroom' and sent the truck skittering across the attic's warped floor, deciding he owed it to the sour little boy who had denied himself the pleasure all those years.

Now that he was middle aged, was he courageous enough to opt for the final solution: throwing the truck into the river? Maybe Sylvia could film it as a performance art piece. Then he had a better idea.

He rushed downstairs and found his mother back from the shops, sitting in the kitchen with Joey, who'd been released from his cage and was perched on a statue of the Child of Prague. All three looked surprised to see Fintan appear out of nowhere brandishing a toy truck.

'Peter left a box behind in the attic.' Fintan's voice crackled with indignation that sounded like the real thing. 'And you'll never guess what I found in it!'

Words Spoken
Aiden O'Reilly

TWO YEARS SINCE HE'S EMERGED FROM ZERO by completing a course in web design, speaking in a clear even tone, and moving into the centre of town to an apartment that leaves him nothing saved at the end of each month. Less than nothing, for his income is supplemented by a claim for rent assistance. No shame in that, none at all; he'd be quite prepared to mention it if the subject came up, but so far it hasn't come up, not among the people he meets now, and there's no reason why it ever should.

He loves to look at the city lights from the top-floor landing. A silent vista through double panes of glass. There is a feeling of contact, of being in the middle of life. The lines of red tail-lights move smoothly, each orange street lamp casts a circular glow on the pavement. The stronger halogen lights around business premises cast a glow on the air itself, creating a fuzz around each intense point. He blinks and rubs his eyes, wondering if the late nights have got to him, or if maybe the shampoo he uses has frosted the corneas. On the corridors and landings there are no windows that open, but when he opens those in his room the air blows in damp and cold, only faintly charged with the fumes of an endless rush hour.

Amanda Bennett invited him. Sure you'll come, it's just people, not my friends. Half of them I'll hardly know, she'd said. You know the way you just invite a load of people because you know only half of them will turn up anyway?

But I'll definitely come, he said.

Right, you know the Bull Harbour building? It's Block E, Apartment

16 but the intercom doesn't work, so I just ask people to give me a buzz as soon as they get to the front door. You have my number, don't you?

Sure, I have your number somewhere, he said.

And you have a mobile?

Yes, I have a mobile, he confirmed in a level voice.

He'd met her in the foyer of Keystroke College where he'd been running an eye down the list of courses starting that month. Do you study here? he'd asked. She pouted, seemed about to say something sharp, then said carefully: Well, I've just finished up a course. Why? Are you thinking of doing one?

He took the cue from her tone. Maybe not, he said, I don't thnk it's that good. Still, it would be nice to have something else on the old CV.

What kind of work do you do?

Graphic design, he answered. He had completed a leaflet for a local karate club just two weeks before. The club rented some warehouse space in his uncle's scrapyard.

Really? she said with interest. Me too! But honestly you'd be better off without the course here. What kind of design work do you do?

Commercial flyers, clubs, that kind of thing.

There's a lot of freelance contracts going around but it's so hard to get anything steady, don't you think?

When they parted she handed him her card as a matter of course, as though he might be another significant contact.

When Amanda comes down the stairs and opens the metal-framed door that evening she's in a different mood, more reckless and trusting, the same confidence, but now it's not based on her professional manner.

Hi, she says, sorry to make you ring. It's just the kids. They hang around outside and press all the buttons. The buzzer went off twice already today. So your doorbell works again?

Yes, but the intercom doesn't, like I said earlier.

The precision of her memory irritates him slightly. He wonders how she can be so involved with every detail that she remembers them all. He follows her up the carpeted stairs, snatching glimpses out the windows, or rather the continuous glass shell, at the tin-can profile of the gasometer and the dark hulk of the stadium. For though he lives in a high apartment himself, he never tires of the transformation from a height, the sudden revelation, like watching your home town become the setting for a Hollywood thriller.

Cathy, Conor, Alvin, Coreen, Louis, Chris. She performs the introductions with six waves of her left hand around the room. Each guest nods and mutters. This is Colin by the way, she adds at the end, I should complete my introductions.

No one offers to shake hands. He figures it's just a mixed party, and wonders how he'll phrase it when they ask him what he works at. But everyone seems content to lounge across the chairs and sofas without conversing much.

Someone has gone to a lot of trouble with the food. Translucent rectangles of smoked salmon on soda bread, grilled cheese on baguette, shredded lettuce and rocket salad, cream cheese on crackers, small cylinders of sushi, bowls of tuna pasta salad, strips of red and green pepper, little sherry-glasses of prawn cocktail with each prawn bent over the rim of the glass, like a man leaning over a railing to puke.

You have a nice apartment, he says.

Don't you want to leave down your coat? she asks. She points him through a door to a second room. He sees a desk and computer. There's a bed with papers and coats thrown across it. Cardboard boxes are wedged between the bed and the wall. Thick hard-backed books stacked on the floor. This is the spare room then; he sees another door opposite which must be her bedroom. A two bed-roomed apartment on a few freelance hours per week. Some things you just have to wonder at and never ask.

Are you still a student? he asks.

No, why? Is it the books lying all over the place? They're just my old ones. I actually go back and read them sometimes.

Not something I'd ever do.

What did you study?

Web design, he answers.

She looks perplexed. But you didn't just do web design?

Indeed I did.

For four years?

What do you mean four years? he asks in a neutral voice, as though he hasn't figured out she assumes he's been to university. As do a lot of people he meets. It's just too unexpected: a presentable professional, or halfway to being a professional, who never went to university. Amanda waits a moment for him to elaborate, then passes into the livingroom.

Take one too, she says, I spent five hours slaving in the kitchen so you'd better appreciate it or you'll never get invited again. She hands him a plate and moves along the table piling on a little of each salad. He would hardly recognise her out of her career-girl slacks. Mousy brown hair you can see the tangles in, mouth too wide and flat. But there's no one going to say this to her, she's too nice for that. She talks on and on in full confidence that talk makes everyone the same, like they are all in the same boat, everything is going to be all right so long as we can keep talking about it. You could introduce yourself with 'I beg for money on Capel Street,' and she'd say, 'Really, you must meet a lot of interesting people. But I wouldn't like to be doing it on a day like this.'

He takes his plate over to the window, where some people are talking about the view. He points out Liberty Hall and the gap where the river lies. It turns into a kind of puzzle, to guess what each significant cluster of lights could be. That stream of lights, he points, is the Stephen's Green Centre. And that chimney there is way over in Smithfield.

In one of the dead ends off the streets directly below is the back entrance he knows too well. It's not true that he's emerged from zero, but the six years after leaving school were spent out of sight in the stockroom of a department store, taking deliveries from lorries. The boxes he stacked were huge, tall as a man, but light. He used a hand-operated hydraulic trolley. Pile on the boxes, raise it up with a few quick pumps of the lever. A forklift wasn't needed, so after all that time in a warehouse he didn't even have a forklift qualification. Not even that one small chance to gain something concrete from his time there. Six years spent in a cavernous space lit with bare bulbs, out back behind the heavy vinyl curtains that separated it from the shop floor. Any new girl who started on the shop floor assumed he must be a grade below them. One who didn't need any training, have to shave or wear a tie, or neat clothes of any sort, and who was incapable of operating a cash register. They were surprised to see he got the same reduction on clothes as everyone else. At Christmas he was handed the same wad of vouchers.

Most of the staff were female—girls straight out of school, mothers with teenaged children, mothers who didn't have any choice. It was the kind of job someone might take up for a few months, despite the impression given by the career opportunities posters around the canteen. People were rotated around the different departments, the bargain basement being the least favourite, even lower than the warehouse. But Colin was never rotated. He regretted not having in his CV the usual line on having experience in dealing with the public. In retrospect, he supposed, there was nobody forcing him to stay hidden out the back. All he'd had to do was ask and he would have been trained at the register. They'd have been happy for him to ask.

But Colin doesn't tell these people about the warehouse entrance below or the empty top floor of the store they could see into through the window. I know the city pretty well from a height, he tells them, you know not a lot of people can figure it out.

Nobody smokes inside the apartment, that's understood. A couple of tiled steps lead down to an aluminium door. Outside is a small terrace, on one side is a drop four storeys to the ground. A gravel oval, two shrubs shrivelled by the wind. The terrace is shared by three other apartments. A clothes rack is tethered to the door frame. Amanda's things flutter brazenly from it.

A guest sitting on the bottom step nods, moves to one side. Cigarette? the man asks, take one of mine. He taps the open end on the packet to firm the tobacco. You don't have to go outside, she allows it here when the door is open.

Not a bad party this.

Yes, Amanda's salads are really—well let's say they're designed to impress, no matter about the taste.

He looks behind himself, ironically checking to see if she is listening. He is in his late twenties, blond hair combed back, the kind of good looks that ease the way through a lot of things. Almost film-star looks, but the accent is familiar. From Dublin anyway.

Where are you from?

Drimnagh.

Not a bad spot.

I haven't lived there for a while, Chris says. This must be Chris, Colin decides, there were a lot of names beginning 'K' introduced around the room.

Nice pad she has here, what? A balcony and the works.

It certainly is, the man replies.

Jays the city out there is a lot different to when I was running into town on the hop from school.

Chris doesn't smile at the chummy language. He speaks like he has to pluck the words from the air.

Things look different. I got used to Canada when I was there.

You were in Canada? I thought you needed a visa for there.

I was there five years, maybe six. Working at various things.

You must've had a brilliant time there. Jays compared to the dump this place was then.

Yes it was great, said the stranger. It was different from Dublin. But it was also in a sense, the loneliest time in my life. A time when I had to come to terms with myself.

Colin can't see where this is going. His heart beats like he's entered a danger zone. Who is this person to say such things? He scrutinises the pale eyebrows and the fingers pointing the cigarette away so the smoke drifts past him. The grey eyes are turned to him, not sharply, but curious, testing. Like he has just told a riddle, and he is not sure if the listener appreciates riddles.

Colin jumps from the step, flicks his cigarette through the half-open door. Fuckin RAIN out there! he says, turns and takes the steps in one bound, rubbing his hands together in feigned anticipation of second helpings.

It's a week of new contacts, new work opportunities in the offing. An email arrives with a few casual sentences:

Hi, Amanda here.

Take a look at this message I got and see if you're interested.

I don't have the time to handle it. You can reply yourself, or
else I can take it on and just pass you the work—I know the
people there and what they want.
>> TCO here at Vigilant. Hi Amanda. Our office would like
to produce a 20–30 page colour document for new clients. I
can't say any more at this stage, but if you are interested in
this project reply asap.

That was how it worked. No fretting about being clean-shaven or
how to knot your tie correctly, no sitting before a table with humble
eyes, no churning up school certificates, hobbies, achievements you are
proud of. The farce of an interview—thinking about the humiliation
brings blood to his face. Two or three in the months after leaving school
had been enough for a lifetime. With this line of work his school results
do not matter, nor does the certificate from his course, which wasn't
even in graphic design. What matters is who you worked for the month
before, what names you can mention. And if it's a name that is
recognised—and in a small country it often is—the job will fall to you.

His old friends, the ones from the department store days and even
earlier, have a laugh at him when they meet. You're your own boss now,
you can lie in the scratcher until two in the afternoon, they laugh, or
rather sneer, for he never meets them intentionally now. They only run
into each other by chance on the streets. There is the usual enquiries
about friends in common: How's old Richie, how's Cully Mac?
Enthusiatic questions, though in fact it is some five or six years since he
has met these other people, and he is not quite sure he would even
recognise them anymore.

They inevitably ask what he's working at these days. He tries to
explain, but it sounds too glib. He doesn't mean to but he gives the
impression that anyone still working on a nine to five job must be a fool.
See you in Fagans sometime, they will say on parting, though nothing
will come of it.

At the end of the week he rings Amanda and asks how the party went.
That party? she says after a pause to figure out he means of course the

one he was at. Sure, it was great. Yeah, he agrees instantly, I really enjoyed it. Thanks for inviting me. He hesitates, he's about to ask casually about one of her guests when she says, I'll let you know when I'm having another one. That would be great, he says, and can't think of any way now to enquire about Chris that wouldn't sound downright weird.

For he had meant to pile a few salads on his plate and go back to the smoking exit, down the three steps. Get talking to Chris some more about Canada, about work there and gun licences, winter snow. Gradually circle back, approach the abruptly severed topic from a different angle.

But it was also in a sense, the loneliest time in my life. The sentence recurs to him at the oddest moments, intriguing him, irritating him. Who did he think he was, this blond-haired man no older than twenty-six, to speak like a teacher, a priest, a prophet? Were the ordinary bullshit words not good enough for him? Maybe it was a sophisticated joke and he'd missed the point. Like the gilt-framed image the guests had passed around at Amanda's that same evening. Bubbling over with laughter, the girls with hand to mouth, then hanging it back up on the wall with ironic reverence. It was a relief of the Sacred Heart. A ring of thorns around the iconic red heart, rays emanating from it. The soft beard and gentle features of the standardised Catholic Jesus. The intense blue eyes followed the viewer from left to right around the room. This was no high technology—just a simple optical illusion. He laughed too, but felt there was some extra hilarity that he'd missed.

Maybe Chris was a student of English, or Arts, and took him for another eternal student in touch with the latest ironies. Maybe it was a scene from some film everybody was supposed to have seen. That would explain the precision of the words spoken, and that little testing smile that seemed to taunt: *Do you recognise this? Who am I being now?*

But it wasn't possible Chris was a student. It didn't fit. He'd mentioned working for six years in Canada. It was understood that 'working' meant ordinary simple jobs, the kind that anyone might get when they need to pay the rent. There isn't a lot to remember and mull over from just two minutes sitting on a step, but everything pointed to complete sincerity, a simple direct statement. But why did he have to speak like that, in a way that sealed off any ordinary reply?

His anger summons back the tiled steps, a man sitting on the bottom one, his grey eyes questioning the smoke curling from a cigarette, an empty pack at his side folded to form an ashtray. Just say what you mean to say, don't make a speech of it, he wants to say in a harsh voice to the stranger who might possibly be called Chris. So you weren't too happy in Canada? Why was that? He speaks in a common-sense tone, forcing the stranger onto his level. He hears about difficulty in finding work, long hours spent in a dead-end job carrying boxes on a building site, a piss-off boss who didn't even know his name. Yeah, he sympathises, a few years of that and you're banging off the walls. You need to have contacts with the right people to get ahead. That's the way it is all over. Did you not try hanging around the Irish bars?

Then the second sentence: *A time when I had to come to terms with myself.*

Fucking queer, Colin rages to himself, springing up from the step again, pacing the room. For what else could the sentence mean? Who else but a gay man would speak like that? What other reason could there be? He's shot through the stomach with anger, not precisely at the possibility that Chris is gay, but the possibility that the words were a lure, testing the waters. And it's not even an anger at being mistaken for gay—on the one occasion that happened before he was only irritated that just because he didn't brag about drinking ten pints at the weekend there must be something odd with his masculinity. All the same, he is resentful, he feels he has uncovered a fraud.

He sits down again at his desk. Pulls a draft guide for mortgage providers in front of him, stares down at it, circles the images he wants moved. His eyes are sore, it's maybe the fifth time he's gotten up and come back with a coffee. Two half-empty cups are perched alongside the monitor, a third is on the floor at his feet. The conversation is waiting to be resumed, there, just to the left of him.

So Chris, he says, sitting down on the step again, slapping a knee. He's a man of the world now, not awkward, not nervous of ambiguities. There are matters to be resolved.

There was something about yourself that you had to change? Something about the way you were? Am I supposed to guess what it is?

Chris smiles, rubs his jaw a bit guiltily. His foot slips on the tiles and bangs against the door. No, I... I was involved in a lot of bad business. Scamming people. You know, knocking at doors pretending to sell insurance, marking the places we could break into later. Nobody would suspect me, Irish you know. It was pretty low stuff.

Jesus.

I had to sort myself out. Big time.

But you got away from it in the end?

Put away from it, he laughs drily, that's how I got away from it. Yeah I didn't stay six years in Canada living the high life, that's for sure. A nice time seeing the world abroad.

I like it, said Amanda on the phone. When you say it took you all day it makes it hardly worthwhile in terms of money, but if you're still on I can pass some more on to you.

Sure, he says brightly.

There's a range of labels we have to adjust to Irish regulations. A Canadian company.

Canadian? There was a Canadian at your party a few weeks ago.

Yes. So there was.

What's he up to?

Up to? Well I suppose he's still putting in heating pumps. He's been in the apartments so many times I just invited him along. But he's very interesting, not at all boring. You'd never guess he was just a plumber.

Another variation: Yeah, "come to terms"? Maybe I don't want to come to terms. Maybe I want to obliterate instead. And the stranger sets his jaw and understands.

But would he really have said that?

It shouldn't be a big surprise to run into Chris one day on the ground-floor corridor of his own apartment building. Yet Colin stops dead. There is something uncanny about the figure, down on his hunkers untying a cable.

Chris? he says uncertainly. Then he sees the tiles are indistinguishable from those at Amanda's building. Chris looks up, there's a moment of recognition untethered to place or time.

What's your name again?

Colin.

Right. Amanda's party. I just have to pack this stuff away. Do you live here?

They head towards the city centre, thinking of some café, but turn in at the doors of a fast-food outlet because they see a couple of free seats inside and it's getting on for lunchtime. He hears about Canada, about the frozen waterfalls, savage winters in Watson Lake, going for a walk through untracked forest and getting lost in the wilderness with the sound of a jam factory whistle cutting the silence every hour, always the same distance away.

Halfway through the coffee a couple of girls come in, throw a glance.

Doyles Stores girls, says Colin, that's the black and white zigzag. The warehouse entrance is up that laneway across the road. We used to come here for our lunch. Three at a time, forty-five minutes. Just enough time to get your food and get it down. I worked there in the stockroom packing boxes for six years.

Six years? Why did you stay there so long?

Colin looks over at the girls in uniform. They are fresh-faced, all laughing, probably still at school just one or two years before. He can't rightly explain why he spent so long there. It seems almost to have been an experiment on himself. He had wanted to see if he could be happy working at a simple job, just living, or if on the other hand something would rebel within him, force him out. It was wrong to make of himself a small and shrivelled thing, wrong to view himself from a height as one more figure walking along the pavement.

It seems to me now like my buried life, he says. Like I wanted to see if I could bury myself under ten feet of earth and be silent and content, or if there was something within me that would make me wake up.

As he speaks it becomes clear that this is what happened, and that the dead self he had dragged along with him could finally be cut loose.

The girls throw a glance back as they pass out the door, but it's not because they recognise him. All the girls from that time would have long since moved on.

The Elephant as a Public Symbol

Maile Chapman

I GO HOME TO FIND MY AUNT TRANSFORMED into my grandmother and my
mother into someone else; she is remarried, and she has a young child,
my half-brother, about five years old by now. I don't know the child
much, and I don't know the child's father at all.

My mother, the child, and I go to see my aunt, who is glad to see me.
The house where my aunt lives hasn't changed at all except for the tea-
towels which she has always had the habit of changing, regularly and
seasonally. Red and green for Christmas. Pink for Valentine's Day. I am
relieved to be there. I love my aunt, and have always known that my
aunt loves me.

I have been away recklessly and overlong, and because of this it is
awkward to be back. My aunt wants to look in my passport to see the
paper trail, because she is interested. She touches all the multi-coloured
stamps. She wants to hear about the ferry to Estonia, and the long trip
overland to St Petersburg, and looks at my name in Cyrillic script on the
golden entry permit pasted in, which looks like my name and yet also
doesn't, proof of another version of me, very far away from here… but
then my mother gets up to go, gathers the child, and tells me it's time to
leave. I thought I was staying with my aunt? Reluctantly, I say goodbye.
My aunt waves and waves from the front steps. Come back anytime, she
says. Soon, even.

We drive and drive, into the city and downtown and then we park
and get out in a shopping arcade. Maybe there is a library in it, upstairs;
this is unfamiliar, all newly built since I went away. My mother says that

there are plans already made ahead of time for the afternoon, the whole afternoon. She doesn't mean me. She is dropping me off at the arcade, where I can presumably amuse myself.

We part suddenly. I am confused. I think they're leaving, and then through one of the big plate glass windows I see them picking their way across the plaza towards the cineplex adjacent. I push through the glass doors and hurry and catch up to them.

Are you going to a movie? I say.

She says, It's a children's movie: it is a *children's movie.*

The child says nothing, looks down, accustomed to letting decisions progress in the air over his head. I turn to save face and go back someplace else. I follow what seems to be a shortcut, the quickest way to disappear. I go into another narrow courtyard between the windowed walls of two big buildings. I'm walking on damp concrete through the supports of a towering work of metal public art; there is a groaning, and the sound of moving air. I am among a herd of steel elephants so large between the buildings that I am walking through their legs under the framework of their lofty bodies. Water moves suddenly. It is a fountain, and the elephants are spraying at random intervals through their skeletal trunks. I can hear the water splashing onto the cement ahead and I understand that although I am to meet them for dinner—the words registering belatedly, that we will meet, *for dinner*—this means that afterwards she will find a way to let me know that I will not be staying with them during this visit, by which time it will be late enough to be hard to find a way back out to my aunt's house without asking my mother to take me there. And my mother might then very well decide that allowing me one night on the couch is less inconvenient than taking me back out there in the car. She must realise that one uncomfortable night on the couch will send me away more handily anyway. She will wake me early. She will feed the child well in front of me, and hardly offer coffee. I will have to ask for a towel, and she will give me an old one with hanging strings. We have done all of this before.

But why didn't she leave me at my aunt's house earlier? My aunt was glad to see me. My aunt wanted to make up the bed for me in the guest room, to thaw frozen strawberries for breakfast in the morning, and to hear everything and to tell me everything, all evening and all morning until eventually I would be on my way again and she would wave goodbye, goodbye, waving from the steps until the next visit.

The public space below the elephants is like all the other places where my mother has dropped me in the past, bus stations and airports, terminals from which anyone can arrive and depart and make their own independent plans and either appreciate or ignore the moment of going. According to her, not every arrival and departure is significant anymore.

I understand, and I can easily remember the candy in her hands now in the darkness of the theatre as she gives it piece by piece to the child. I can picture the reddish flip of her hair illuminated, carefully done, even if I manage to forget, in the intervals, that her priorities are a mystery.

I am sad. But wait, wait, wait: I remember that my aunt has become my grandmother and that I want to spend as much time with her as possible while I am here; she won't care about offending my mother by taking me in. My mother is someone else now anyway; why should I kill time waiting for her? She'll be fine, she has the other child with her, watching cartoons in the dusty darkness of a sunlit afternoon. When they come out into the plaza she will have forgotten me. I don't know what I was thinking. Am I not flexible? Am I not resourceful? I can do anything. It is no challenge at all for me to strike out through the crowds of the plaza and buy a ticket and find and board a bus going in the right direction. It will be easy, very easy; my aunt is probably already expecting me.

tourbusting4

Toby Litt

THERE'S THIS MOMENT—and if you're lucky enough to be in a half-decent band, you'll know it.

It comes when you're playing a gig, can be near the start but never right at the start, can be during an encore, but usually it comes halfway through the second verse of one of your best—for some reason not your *very* best—songs.

You stand there, playing whatever instrument you play, with me it's drums, and at the same time you're able to sit way way the fuck out towards the very back of your mind—and you're able to watch everything around you.

The music isn't exactly playing itself, but during that moment it feels just like it could, possibly, with one more push.

And sometimes, just then, when this is upon me, someone else in the band will feel the exact same thing at the exact same moment, and they'll turn sideways from the audience, and we'll exchange a glance that says it all.

And after this moment, whether there's been a glance or not, what I always feel is best is to look out into the audience—if the lighting allows—and find someone there that saw the glance and understood just what it meant: that this, for us, isn't just another gig, this is the reason we go through all the other shit in the first.

There is a moment—I know there is a moment; I remember it pretty well, it's just, it's been so long since I've experienced it, since I've made any kind of eye contact with another member of *okay*. (Our image doesn't exactly require us to be chummy-chummy. I know that certain fansites have compiled lists of the gigs we broke off halfway through, after throwing our instruments at one another's heads or feet.)

This, the above, is why I thought it was time to tour again—not, I repeat, *not* for the money; there is enough of that, given our back catalogue and the eventual decision to let them use 'Sea Song' to advertise that cranberry juice.

No, I wanted to feel the moment, be in it, and then do a little dance around its precinct.

I'm thirty-five now, and I've only got a limited number of little dances left—or a limited time in which to dance them, without loss of dignity. (Dignity, surprisingly, is important to me—even the controlled loss of it: children bring this upon one.)

When I dance these days bits of me move that never used to, because they were never there, or because they were more securely attached.

I don't want to be an embarrassment to anyone, least of all my daughters who will see the footage when they grow up—but I *do* need, for what feels like the last time, in California-speak, to reconnect.

And so I called Syph, and I called him, and I called again, and after a week, when he probably thought I was his dealer, he picked up.

'Hey,' he said, a hey which seemed to go on for at least ten seconds.

Although we are famous together, and I am one quarter of the reason he is (as lead singer) ten times more famous than I am, it took me a minute to get him to show any comprehension of who I was.

'Oh,' he said, 'hi.' He wasn't unfriendly, he was just speaking long-distance, and not to me, to his own mouth—I could tell; I knew him and his drug moods well enough. It was anti-depressants with God knows what layered on top: drugs of focus, drugs of obliteration—a careful balance that no longer worked, certainly not for me, probably not for him.

I explained what I was thinking—a tour of smaller venues—and Syph didn't say no: whether he'd still remember this conversation the time after the next time he lost consciousness... I decided to fax him a reminder, then called the others.

Mono was out of the house, probably fishing with Major. Since she quit the perfume counter and moved in to his lakeside shack, that's mostly what they've done—apart from have three children (could be a problem). I left a message on his machine, faxed, emailed and wrote him a letter on fluourescent paper, just so I could be sure.

Crabs picked up after a ring and a half. He doesn't move far from the phone, ever, and is probably keeping that close so as to be sure he doesn't miss exactly *this* call, when it comes. He lives for the road and dies without it. 'I'll be there,' he said, before I'd even said where.

L.A.—two weeks later. Crabs having taken the red-eye, gone to hang out with Syph and try to get him both straight and in the mood. Mono having had the letter, and the fact that he owned an answerphone, a fax and a computer, drawn to his attention by the delightful Major. Perhaps she wanted him out of the house. Now I see what made Syph fall for her—she's a solid woman. She'd put any man right, even Syph.

Not like the matchstick I found him with when I arrived at his off-Mulholland (please, don't do it, Syph—but I just love the view) mansion. I can never remember who it used to belong to, but they were very famous and waited till they'd moved out before drinking themselves to death. Syph wasn't intending to make the same mistake. The windows were painted black, I saw from the outside, and also covered with tinfoil, I saw when I cleared a space on the couch and sat down—very grateful not to have spiked myself on a needle, of which there were many. I hadn't known it was this bad. Crackhouse chic—burns up some of the walls, Jackson Pollocks of dried blood, a sea of takeout containers, mice. It can be a terrible thing, when the cheques keep coming in without you having to go out of the house. Syph was wearing the darkest pair of glasses I've ever seen.

I remembered wanting The Moment back, but I also wanted to save my friend from himself, from the matchstick girl, the drugs, the guy in an expensive leather jacket in the shadows.

Crabs had got Syph onto the JD, so he was at least not raging. Whilst I talked, he did what passes with a lead singer for listening: wait for the sentences that include his name and then follow the content from then until the next period is reached. I had long known how to deal with this, and so began every other sentence with, 'If Syph agrees...' or 'Syph, of course, is important here for...' This pisses both the others off, but they know it has to be done—otherwise decisions are reached that Syph later claims never to have been consulted about. Legally, this causes problems, worst of all was the cranberry juice ad.

I told Syph that Syph had been really fired up by the idea of a small-scale tour, first time I called Syph, and Syph seemed to believe me. The other two knew I was lying but didn't mind; checking with them later, I confirmed that, seeing the state our old friend was in, they'd decided to join me on my mercy mission: get him road-ready, get him away from all the leather jackets and matchgirls.

'We'll just turn up in a van,' I said. 'Let the college radio station hear about it, accidentally, a few hours before. Appear under a different name, play covers, or hardcore versions of our songs, or whatever the fuck we want.'

'Whatever the fuck we want,' said Syph, with a smile, then nodded off. I'd forgotten to include his name in that last sentence.

We had made a start. The following afternoon, the band reconvened. Syph was very different—completely lucid, focussed, aggressive and wanting to be in charge. From what he said, it appeared he now believed that he'd called us together, that the small-scale tour was his idea and that, out of the other three, I was the one being obstructive.

'Er, Syph,...' said Mono, but I shook my head at him. Although delusional, this was fine—I didn't mind Syph misquoting me; better that than dying before our eyes.

Syph had been up all night. Our management, who I was interested to find were still interested in us, had taken an early morning flight down from Toronto—were due to arrive within an hour.

'They'll deal with all the shit,' said Syph, who hadn't sat down once since we arrived. 'The bookings, the fees, the equipment.'

'Of course they will,' Mono said. 'That's their job.'

'And we can just...' said Crabs. He closed his eyes, nodded and mimed a descending bass part that I think I recognised.

'Fucking *exactly*,' screeched Syph. 'They can talk, we can rock!'

I remembered a time, long ago, when we only used the word *rock* ironically—verb or noun, it didn't matter; the word referred to something bands did to please fans who made satan fingers back at them. When I looked at Syph, now on the point of raging, I realised what a Monster of Rock really was. I also realised exactly what kind of price, in terms of personal humiliation, I was going to have to pay to save Syph's life—or temporarily delay his death. The management should be doing all this.

The management arrived. I won't describe them, they are scum on a percentage—scum on the skim. They talked almost exclusively to Syph, and once they were over the disappointment of not making the maximum amount of money possible, they began to agree with everything he said. Weirdly, Syph gave them my speech of the day before, about why we should do this tour—word for fucking word. I didn't think he had that kind of memory left. Mono looked at me and shook his head, Crabs didn't. They nodded and smiled and said absolutely and sipped drinks that contained no caffeine.

'We need somewhere to rehearse,' said Syph, and one of them made a note in his palm.

Five days later, we were in some purpose-built studio with everything we might want—especially everything Syph might want. Men in expensive leather jackets came and went throughout the afternoon, and Syph spoke to them in a unisex toilet with more horizontal than vertical mirrors.

'It's comfortable,' said Mono, lying on a long leather couch. I didn't know whether he meant the couch, the studios or our life in general.

Syph banged out of the bathroom. 'Okay,' he shrieked, 'let's rock'n'roll!'

We picked ourselves up and moved slowly across to our instruments. I have to say, it was good to be reunited with our old equipment. It had been a year and a half. My kit had been lovingly treated by my personal hi-grade drum-tech—the last I'd seen of it, it was scattered across the stage of some arena. We in *okay* don't usually trash our instruments, but it was the end of the tour and I wanted to shock everyone into listening to my 'I quit' announcement. They did, they just didn't take it seriously—it's horrible when your friends know you really well.

Horrible, but great sometimes, too. From the moment the bass intro to the first song started up, we were *okay* again. No matter how many sessions I do with other musicians (it pays well), there is something fated about how we work together—as a rhythm section, as a band, as a sound. I looked around for someone to make eye contact with, but Mono and Crabs were entirely heads down at work—and Syph was working an imaginary audience.

We played through our setlist, with smiles, jokes and sips from Cokes in between. Syph only went to the bathroom twice, and we accommodated this by jamming whilst he was away and kicking into fast numbers the moment he came back through the door, raging. Part-band, part-nurse.

I tried to ignore the management, who stood somewhere off to our left—nodding, as if they liked music. We sacked our first manager because he wasn't getting us bookings on television, and never since had we dealt with anyone in possession of an undamned soul. Oh, we made so many mistakes—and this, I was beginning to feel, was another of them.

'Come round to my room,' I whispered to Mono and Crabs at the end of the rehearsal, 'about one o'clock.' We were all staying in the same hotel, so they didn't have to cross town or anything.

'What is it?' said Crabs, who joined me and Mono around quarter of two. Mono, thank God, hadn't asked me anything—I think he knew already. We had just sat and watched a movie, buddies.

'I don't think we should tour,' I said.

'The fuck, man,' Crabs said.

'It won't help,' I said.

'I agree,' said Mono.

'The tour was your idea,' said Crabs.

'It was,' I said. 'But this,' I gestured around the tasteful beige interior and out over the grid of L.A. lights, 'this wasn't.'

Crabs said, 'Yes, but—'

And Mono said, 'Clap is right. We're not helping Syph. This isn't what he needs. It's turning into a monster already.'

'*He's* turning into a monster,' I said.

After the rehearsal, we had gone back to his house to celebrate. Without him making a single call, people began to arrive for the party, none of them had to ask where the bathroom was, and by the time I left, about a hundred were there. I was surprised Crabs had remembered our meeting, or thought it urgent enough to attend. Perhaps there was something still in there.

'It's turning into whatever,' said Crabs. 'I don't care. I just want to play.'

'So do I,' I said. 'That's why I started this—if you remember. But we've lost that before we've even started. We can't just *do* anything any more.'

'We're not real,' said Mono. 'We've stopped being real. This isn't real.'

'It's true,' I said. He had put it too well—it was the sort of comment that changes your life. These days, I tried to avoid hearing those.

'Well, fuck, yeah, hey, man, we're keeping it real for our brothers on the street.' Crabs was more drunk or something than I'd noticed. 'We were never *real*.'

'We tried to be,' said Mono. 'At least, I thought we tried. What have we got left to be true to?'

Mono said: 'The music. The fans.' Because it was something he would say in an interview, we knew it was a lie.

'Each other,' I said. Mono had been saying everything I'd meant to say, and better than I could have said it, right now. Major had trained him well. I needed to put in at least one comment that went in advance of him.

'We are,' said Crabs.

'Syph needs help,' said Mono. 'He doesn't need more drugs and fun. He needs to lead a very boring life, supervised by people who are paid lots of money to make him forget he's bored.'

'We can talk to him,' said Crabs.

'God can talk to him, perhaps,' said Mono. 'He won't listen to anyone else.'

'So it's all over. We just pack up and go home and wait for this to happen again in a year's time.'

'No,' Mono said, 'we stay here—at least, one of us stays here to be around Syph. We try to get him through.'

'Yes,' I said. 'That's what we should do.'

After a long while, Crabs said: 'I disagree.' Then he walked out.

Mono and I stayed in my room and decided to do what needed to be done.

The management had been partying with Syph, or pretending to party, but they were up and bright at ten o'clock when Mono and I made a surprise visit to their L.A. office. We explained our position to them, and watched them cope first of all with the idea that we might be important enough to interfere with their plans (a three-month itinerary already roughed out on the wall), then with the fact we were asking them to behave like responsible adults and finally that there were very good reasons, even of profit, why they had to admit we were right. They agreed to nothing, formally—but they said they'd see what they could do. We left, aware we'd have to fire them pretty soon, and that it would take money and lawyers and more money.

We went for lunch, then drove to the rehearsal rooms together. Mono had hired a Mustang of some sort, I don't know cars. It was red and made a boom of blissful bass. The sun was shining in a blue sky on grey roads and off-white buildings. I wasn't tempted for a moment.

In the parking lot was an ambulance. We ran towards it, expecting to find Syph in a coma

We'd only got about halfway there when two men got out of the cab, walked round and opened the back doors of the ambulance.

It was Syph, on a gurney but fully conscious—raving. Beside him, crying, was the matchgirl.

'No,' she said.

'What's this?' asked Mono.

'Hi,' said Syph, pushed up onto an elbow.

'He refused to go to hospital,' matchgirl said. 'He made them bring us here.'

'Rock'n'roll,' Syph said, and grinned—his eyelids were twitching, there was no flesh on his face.

'Is this true?' Mono asked one of the ambulance guys.

'He said to bring him here. He said he felt fine.'

'Half an hour ago, he stopped breathing,' the girl said.

'I think I'm going to write a song about it,' Syph said. 'I've got the chorus.'

The management came out through reception, followed by Crabs. 'What's going on here?' the management asked.

'And you brought him here?' said Mono, very angry.

'He insisted,' said the same ambulance guy. 'And he promised us tickets.'

'What if he died?' I asked. 'Your tickets wouldn't be much good then.'

The ambulance guy smiled as if he knew better, which he probably did.

'I'm not going to die,' said Syph, 'I just want to go and play some music.'

'Hey, man,' said Crabs, 'are you okay?'

'Never better,' said Syph. 'Breezy.' He sniggered. 'Can I have some more of that oxygen?'

The matchgirl put her huge face in her huge hands and her tiny body bounced with sobs.

I turned to the management. 'He needs to go to the hospital, immediately.'

'We need to think about this,' said one of the management.

'No, you don't,' said Mono. 'You need to make sure your number one client doesn't die.'

'What do you want?' the other half of the management asked Syph.

'Like I said, man…'

The management took a step or two away, to consult in private.

It was then that the girl shrieked, 'He went blue! He stopped breathing and I didn't know how to make him start again. I didn't know. He was blue all over.'

'I'm okay,' said Syph.

'I just hit him on the chest, like they do on the TV.'

'Thank you,' said Mono. 'We're very grateful. You did exactly what you should.'

'You'll definitely get tickets,' said one of the management. 'Backstage pass, too.'

The girl held Syph's hand. 'I love your music.'

'He goes to hospital,' said half the management while the other half made a call.

'Thanks, babe,' said Syph, to the girl. He lay back and closed his eyes.

'Do your job,' said Mono to the ambulance guys. 'We'll follow you.'

'What do you want?' the guy asked Syph.

'He's doing it again,' sobbed the girl.

'No, I'm not,' Syph said.

'Give him some oxygen, for Christ's sake,' I said.

'Are you taking him here?' asked the management making the call and pointing to the address on the side of the ambulance.

'Who are you phoning?' asked Mono, in the management's face. 'The *L.A. Times* or *Music Week*?'

'The publicity department,' the other management said. 'They always handle this kind of thing.'

Mono turned to Crabs. 'How fired are these fuckers?'

'Very fucking fired,' said Crabs.

Management looked at me, their last chance.

'Third vote,' I said. 'You're out. I never want to see you or hear from you again.'

'You'll hear from our lawyers,' the management said, both together.

Crabs got in the back of the ambulance and one of the guys closed the door on him and the matchgirl, whose name it later turned out was Celia.

Management walked away. The siren started up—and I wondered how much extra that would cost us. Didn't matter. It was worth it.

I looked at Mono and he looked at me, and that look said it all.

We walked together towards the big red car.

Another Map
Jennifer Brady

EVERY NIGHT IN THE RESTAURANT, the lobsters are boiled alive, the shark meat seared with the rib of the grill. I never see how they do that, the chefs, never get that close, but I see where it all where it all ends up. I see the guts on the kitchen floor, the meat hooks reeking on the wall, hooks strong enough to hold a body. They hold all sorts there. Everything and anything.

I came to Long Island to work all summer, to pay for coming here to work all summer. Don't have a visa, can't get a job that pays enough for a flight home earlier. But, I will leave sooner either way. I have no desire to work in this restaurant, this town, this place, anymore.

I want to go home.

I never heard of a bus person before I came to the States, but that's what they call me, the bus person, which is someone who carries the plates and glasses and other things in and out of the kitchen all night. Not a waitress yet. Don't have the skills for that. Get the panics when there's too much to think about at any one time. Bussing is fine, bussing will do. I do what I'm paid to do. Help customers through meals, replace dropped forks, mop up spilt wine, balance leftovers in trays on my hip. I carry the trays back and forth to the kitchen all night, passing them to the porters, three of them, who coo endearments and pinch their fingers near my groin, *pssssh, pssssh*.

Gato they call me and I keep my eyes away from them. They don't speak my language. I don't speak theirs. The clean bus bins are stacked on the lowest shelf near the head porter, a large-bellied man, whose only job seems to be to polish the knives.

Last night, when the customers and the chefs were gone, I went to the kitchen to collect the last of the trays. When I stooped to get the tray, the head porter, still polishing his knives, purred *muy bien chica* as if I bent for him and him alone. *Bueno* he murmured when I straightened up. His voice was hoarse. When I turned around the three of them were looking at each other, confirming something, and the ratty one with the tash peeked through the kitchen door, solid chrome, like a freezer door with a big airtight latch. He kicked it shut and stood in front of it. They don't speak my language. I don't speak theirs. I strayed into their world—dumb animal, got caught up in their kitchen of bones and blood.

It took a while to walk to Kirk Avenue where I share an apartment with seven people I hardly know. I sat on the steps of the veranda and opened a beer. The sky was like a pool of tar, the stars sitting in it like bits of scalp, making my head burn when I looked at it. I heard snoring from inside. I heard the couple from Belfast shifting on the floor, grunting. I stared at the blackness above. My hands shook, yet I felt calm. It was my neck that hurt, and under my arms too. The other parts were numb. My apron was still tied around my waist, the top part had fallen down and was hanging over my stomach like a patch. I fumbled in the pockets and found a stubbed out cigarette, a book of matches. I lit the stubber and drew the smoke deep into my lungs. As I exhaled I imagined taking the knife out of the porter's hand and sinking it into his belly and emptying the guts out of him. I imagined skating in his blood on the clean tiles, I imagined the flies buzzing on the ultraviolet bars of the flytrap, straining for a hatching spot in his spilt appetites. When I finished the cigarette all I wanted to do was sleep.

I prayed no one was in my sleeping bag and that the strip of carpet behind the sofa was free. I found used earplugs in a side-pocket of my rucksack to block out the snores and the grunts and the other sounds… *pssssh, pssssh. Gato. Muy bien chica. Bueno.*

When the sun came through the veranda doors I felt like I was laid out in gold. A creature znitzed past my nose and the first things I saw when I opened my eyes were its wings of ghoulish muslin, the sun not so golden after all, pressing weakly through them, reminding me something was rancid.

I got the fly from God for a reason, and I battered it dead with a flip-flop. My heart started pounding. I ran to the shower and stood under the water for half an hour, ignoring the banging on the door from my flatmates who cursed me and stomped off to work.

I went to the beach to rid myself of the smells and sounds, they clung to me no matter how much I scrubbed and soaked and prised.

The fishermen who trawl for the restaurant and deliver the shark and lobsters to the kitchen always tell me: never go swimming when the sea is grey. You end up swollen and swallowed by sharks. You end up back in the kitchen.

There was no one in the ocean now because the weather was turning and the sea was grey, but my body ached, my armpits red from the hoisting where I was hung from the rim of the T-shirt, the apron neck-loop too fragile, snapped and dropped me too low for them. I wanted to be taken from the everything and anything, and go to the dark of the ocean.

I loved the sea today, all jam like, jelly they call it here. Grape-jelly sort of grey. But today it was the jam from home, viscous, turbulent, you could lie on it and it would suck you in and you'd willingly go, it looked so easy, you'd go in a minute, down on that old lumpy mattress, something shabby, something from home, and I wanted to go home so badly, with the weather turning and the Atlantic all nasty again, it reminded me of home beaches, all stone and chill, and the familiarity of the big wave crashing, and I saw the wave on the other side, and I saw them fishing out my body, leaving it on my parents' doorstep, my mother putting me to bed, her hand on my forehead, her wedding ring loosening, falling into my eye socket, her fingers thinner than they should be.

I waded in, the waves massive, but I was not scared. They did not pull me down. A riptide did. It grabbed my ankles and dragged my feet along the bed of the sea until there was nothing under my soles. Then the waves swept me into their ruffles and swung me around. They danced with me until the beach was far away. When I opened my eyes I saw the shore as a strip of yellow ribbon in the white sky. At that moment I realised I was not alone, that there was someone in here with me. I saw his spread-eagled figure through a wave like a pressed flower rolling towards me and over me.

I never saw his face, but he had a very strong arm with blond hairs matted in paisley-shaped swirls, and when the arm closed around my neck I rested my lips on it, I hooked my claws in, one set on the forearm, the other on the bicep and I coughed my guts up on those swirls, hocked up the salt, which I swallowed and re-swallowed as the waves shoved us face down then yanked us back up, as if by the hair, to breathe for seconds, before flexing a bigger muscle, bulgier than the last, filling our bodies with its own blood.

The man sounded young, young enough not to be somebody's father. I hope he was not somebody's father. I hope he had the red shorts. The red shorts were important to me and I think I felt them behind me as he treaded against the back of my legs. I felt they were red. It is better if he was just doing his job. I have to believe that they were red. He tightened his grip on my neck and I choked. When he spoke, he spoke gently. He asked me what my name was and could I count to three.

I told him about the sun in the morning and the fly I killed and about the kitchen and the big solid door that shut tight and that I couldn't see my mother's face or my family at all and I felt bad that if they ever find out it was not them I was thinking of in these last moments, they would be upset.

He told me we were to play a game. He wanted me to count to three and every time we got to three, to hold my breath, hold on to him, and never, never to look back. All I had to worry about was the counting and holding, the counting and holding.

Listen to me, he said. The waves are too big to swim against, we need to go with them. Don't panic or we're both dead.

I nodded.

We're aiming for there, he said, and his free arm gestured

somewhere diagonally, it was hard to see how far exactly—my hair was stuck to my face and my eyes stung, they stung all those miles away and not seeing made me wish for the route I knew best.

The shore directly ahead, the golden ribbon of land.

From here to there, he shouted, is an angle. We're going to float in sideways and get there eventually. It will take time, be calm.

I remembered with a shock of pain my father explaining trigonometry homework till ten in the evening, me red in the face, hating him, hating the agoraphobia of being lost along the monstrous triangle arms that closed up corners where angles hid—angles that indicated infinities. I remembered the appearing and disappearing of logic, and my father exasperated, his head in his hands: *Let me explain it again.* It occurred to me that the diagonal distance may be not so impossible after all, that there was a science to getting back to shore—the angle could work and I heard my father shouting, *Use your intelligence,* but I heard it like a prayer and I wished I had the chance to sit with him once more and learn it again for real, because the triangles I drew in the sea kept turning into straight lines and I couldn't see any angle anymore. I just couldn't see it.

I started for the land directly ahead. The man tightened his grip on my neck. I felt him peddling hard behind me, but not as hard as before. I knew he was losing his strength and felt him tugging me down. I kicked him and he held on to my arm until the next wave came. We both went under and that was the last time I felt him or saw him, but I heard a whimper making its way to the surface of the sea, as if it came from a bag of grit, and the whimper got louder and I couldn't bear the screams I heard, under that sea.

The voices of the fishermen are telling me, never go swimming when the sea is grey. You'll end up drowning and swollen and swallowed by a shark. You'll end up back in the kitchen. You come back either way. I hear them laughing.

They say that drowning is the nicest way to go. It takes two minutes, or five, they say, then it feels all floaty-floaty—a dream-off drift-off. Better not think of that. Get the panics when there's too much to think about at any one time.

When I get to land, I will ring home. This time they will answer, this time they will send the money. I am going to pay for a flight back, to see the Atlantic from the other side again and see my mother's face to remind me that I came from somewhere, that there was another map with a place for me waiting on it.

The Complicated Architect

Ronan Doyle

THE SMALL STATION'S PLATFORM WAS CROWDED. Pigeons gathered on the beams above and one young man gaped at his watch. The people around me became anxious, coughing and shuffling their feet. Then the train was before us and the doors hissed open.

I took a seat by a window in the smoking compartment. I put my plant on the floor. A thin woman and a boy with large eyes sat down opposite me. She brushed some hair from her eyes, lit a cigarette and stared out the window. I needed to shower, or at least to wash my hands and face.

The train backed out of the station. I looked at the lines of iron and steel, at the wires in the air and the receding blocks of mortar. In my jacket pocket the slight weight against my chest reminded me that, in reality, much was wrong. We passed into a tunnel. Light streaked the wall and the boy started to whimper. The woman looked at him. Then she looked at me. She turned back to the window and drew long from the cigarette. I closed my eyes and tried to remember exactly what had happened.

***

When I arrived at the apartment he was marking out on the wooden floor the areas within which I could move. I stood there, watching him crawl backwards on all fours, and sensed the sun sliding down behind the mountain.

His work soon completed he raised himself slowly and hung the chalk and string on a nail inside the door. Then he joined me outside to look at the sky. He was a weary looking creature, lean and just too short to have an effect.

'It is very beautiful,' he said.

And indeed it was, even if I knew that from the balcony on the other side all we would see was the grey-blocked, stretching-away city.

We remained there a few minutes in silence admiring the counter-view. Soon the sun had gone away and there was that time when the mountains go black and the crest is a red line against the dark blue sky. I observed a few shots of white light moving up through the falling clouds.

'Oh, my teeth!' he exclaimed abruptly. 'What confusion they have caused.'

I did not repay this outburst with the indifference it deserved.

'What of your teeth?' I asked.

He looked directly at me and I recognised that a blunder of some kind had been made.

'They're yellow,' he replied rather sullenly, parting his lips in a grimace like an animal. Or perhaps this was his smile. Either way, I recoiled, impulsively.

His teeth were a little yellow, it's true, but they were aligned and well-shaped, and I had not noticed the discolouration. What was wrong with him?

'Your teeth are fine,' I said, and suggested that we go inside. It was, in fact, becoming a little cold.

I removed my shoes, placed them by his and stepped into the small kitchen, carrying my briefcase.

Then I studied the fine white track drawn out upon the floor. The toilet and shower, small compartments on my immediate left, were evidently for communal use, as the line commenced beyond them. Everything to the left of the line, he informed me, was mine—an arrangement denying me the fridge, cooker and one side of the kitchen table, though not the sink. From the table the line continued for five or six feet to the adjoining *tatami* room, which, later, would be divided by a screen. Mine, he said, was the half on the left. Later a futon would be thrown down beside a small, low-lying pouffe near the balcony window.

I understood that I had been allotted the minimum space necessary to survive. And the pouffe was a luxury that I would need to manipulate.

He offered me a drink.

In the kitchen he broke ice with a steel spike and more than ever I felt the stranger.

'You will stay for a week,' he said, walking into his half and sitting down in the *seiza* position. He was not Japanese and I found it unsettling that he chose to sit this way.

'Ten days,' I replied, using the briefcase on my lap as a table for my drink. I looked at him, trying to note the physical effect of my words. But his face didn't change at all. For a minute there was nothing except the clink-click sound of melting ice.

He enquired after my sister. I explained that I had not spoken to her in almost two years, not until that recent conversation on the phone. I said that I appreciated what he and my sister were doing for me. But the rest I had left behind a long time ago.

'I love your sister very much,' he said quite solemnly and staring at me, as if his eyes would explain everything.

I merely nodded, in a dumb fashion. And then I was outside myself, in a high place looking down at the other nodding like that. I could not relate to the emotions responsible for the gesture.

We sat in further silence. I on the pouffe, he on the floor.

'Ten days can be the longest time,' he said, after a while. I did not feel in a position to disagree, and it was true that already the minutes were slowing down. I could hear clearly the deregulated hands of a clock that I could not see. The sound reminded me of waiting in holy places or of large, empty rooms.

'But I think that segregation will help us,' he said, motioning towards the lined floor with a lazy hand, smiling with his lips and yellow teeth.

'Why should we encourage the clattering together of two strangers?'

In spite of the severity of the measure I found myself agreeing with him again. Nothing seemed too ludicrous.

'Of course, you've had a tiring day,' he told me. It was best that I turn in for the night.

He pulled across the sliding door. It had a wooden frame with paper skin. On it, for decoration, a mountain landscape cast in pale green and blue and yellow colours, a few unfamiliar birds tearing off in the distance. I heard him pull up a chair and sit down at the table in the kitchen. He groaned then, and the light from the kitchen fell upon my door, making it softly glow.

At some point I had a dream.

Which I don't recall, but when I opened my eyes breathing quickly, my T-shirt sticking to the skin beneath my arms, I saw a large rat sitting on the pouffe. It was a rat, sure enough, with a tough dark body and hard, curling tail and, of course, the eyes that shined yellow, the nose that scratched the air, the protuberant teeth. Not until I reached up and pulled the light cord did it disappear. Or rather, the absence that I had believed to be a rat revealed itself.

I saw my face reflected in the window's black glass. It would be difficult to sleep. Then the phone rang into the stillness and I moved swiftly to turn out the light and lie down, pretending to be asleep.

Hearing him answer I immediately felt foolish.

'That was your sister,' he called, and then seemed to hang there, waiting for my reply. I confess I was furious that he had realised I had been awake, and resentful that he had chosen to let me know he had realised.

He was at the sink, running the tap, and I imagined him leaning over with outstretched arm, the sucked-in chest, taking care not to violate my space with his feet. Something stirred in me then, perhaps it was lunacy, spinning its round. Or perhaps it was something less spectacular. I began to imagine various complex operations involving broom handles, skewers and tape, plundering cheese and meat from the fridge without crossing the line. I laughed softly to myself, the only man who could truly understand the joke. And what an odd man he was, I thought.

What time was it? I noticed that the clock's noise was normal again.

And I was suddenly quite angry, given the whole situation.

Some time later, I understood that I had been staring at the ceiling for a length of time I could only trace back to the source of anger. Which lingered, slowly festering. The *shoji* had been pulled across in the Japanese manner, dividing the *tatami* rooms for our privacy. From the adjoining space I could hear my sleeping host. I cannot, even now, truthfully claim that he was snoring. No, his was the unmistakably wholesome respiration known only to those who forget the world when they close their eyes. The sound of a contented body labouring independently of thought.

About the point where I had been staring, a spherical radiance had illuminated itself upon the ceiling and the darkness. And for some time this illusion had been slowly pulsating and growing, regulating itself to the steady in-and-out of the other's breathing. I began to believe that I was suffocating and found myself in reality clutching weakly at my throat.

When I sat up the light vanished and after a few moments the sound of him sleeping was precisely as before. I waited, sitting in my room, listening and waiting for my eyes to adjust to the darkness.

At the kitchen sink I let the tap run slowly so that he might not hear. Beyond the mountains light was gathering in a corner of the night. I drank the water slowly and it was not cold enough. My feet were too cold, having stepped from the relative warmth of the *tatami* mat onto the long coolness of the kitchen floor. I left the glass on the draining board.

Then, without forethought, I took the chalk and string from the nail and held it in the palm of my hand. It was very white there. The string slipped off my palm and pointed me towards the floor. I looked around the silent, empty kitchen and promptly fell to my knees.

With a damp cloth I carefully cleaned away the white chalk markings leading to the sink. I waited a few moments, and then, when the floor had dried, I gave it a good shine with the tea-towel. I extended my allotment by a mere six or seven inches, sufficient so that he could not reach the sink at all. Then I returned to my room clutching my stomach, trying desperately not to laugh aloud.

When I lay down my heart was thumping hard. I ate the pillow until I relaxed and there wasn't a sound in the apartment except a bird or two outside, chirping like soothing, feminine creatures. The inside of my head seemed like a part of the ocean, like a long, solitary branch in a damp, green field. I fell asleep without difficulty and did not wake until the sun was high in the sky and shedding its tepid light upon the room in fat and yellow slabs.

In the shower I reviewed what I had done the night before and the day seemed promising, although I also felt uneasy, there being the likelihood that my handiwork would be identified.

I opened my briefcase and selected a clean pair of underpants. The tag inside the waistband chaffed uncomfortably against my skin. I walked about the room, at once massaging the small square of offended skin at my lower back and trying to adjust the tag so that it might not annoy me so. The manoeuvre proved hopeless. Soon I understood that I would certainly be confronted about what I had done the night before and this sense of hazard completely overrode my previous satisfaction.

I noted with distaste the clear droplets on my white and pimpled shoulders, the clear morning light on my flesh and the pale hanging bag of my belly.

'Would you like some eggs?' he called loudly from the kitchen.

His voice was a shock and on impulse I protected myself directly, one arm covering the belly-bag, my knee drawn up around the groin and my other arm crooked across the chest, a claw on my shoulder.

'Yes, yes I *would* like some eggs!' I cried, my voice as fragile as the day itself. In the centre of the room I stood alone on one foot, a stork clown. Collecting myself and closing the briefcase—which made a distinct snap—I hastily dressed and strolled into the kitchen.

'Sleep well?' he enquired.

'Like a baby,' I replied.

He was cracking eggs into a large blue bowl. Bread and cheese, ham and sliced tomato were set out. Salt and pepper and herbs. The smell of coffee heating in a steel espresso maker on the stove.

'Put a little water in this,' he said, passing me the bowl of eggs without looking up.

I immediately understood it was a trap, and a droplet of sweat that had been clinging to my underarm detached itself and slid coolly down my side.

'Yes, water,' I said, taking the bowl to the sink. I resolved there and then to deny the whole affair if questioned. But just then I saw his head reflected in the shiny curved tap. It was grotesque and warped and large in the middle, his neck and crown stretched out to appalling silver lines. Seeing him like this enraged me. I was even angry with myself for having been so tense and bothered.

I turned and thrust back the bowl, perhaps too violently. Its contents splashed when I set it down upon the table.

He looked up and smiled, choosing to ignore the situation.

'Hungry?' he asked.

I said that I was starving.

The day passed as others. I felt myself moving nowhere in particular. I walked around the apartment block. Then straight up a narrow, dusty road and I crossed the railway line. I went along for a while by small wooden houses, up a smaller brick lane, by drink and cigarette machines hooked into the walls and a red lantern hanging outside a nondescript restaurant. I turned around and for an instant felt completely lost. The world seemed to pile in around me, buildings leaned over, the lane closed in, a furious cat appeared on a wall-top, brandishing its claws. I went straight back the way I had come and crossed the railway line and the top of the tall apartment building came into view.

After taking a second shower, I gazed at myself in the mirror without a thought in my head. He was in the kitchen, typing at his computer. He had said that he worked from home. I suspect he also thought himself a writer, but I doubted he had the bottle for it. A low-level academic at most. His fingers tapped and tapped the keys, a little man in a white cap chipping at a piece of rock.

I dried myself slowly and carefully. I sat in the pouffe by the balcony window and put my hands on my knees. I opened my briefcase and took out my book and read a few chapters at random. I put the pages back in the briefcase and then I took out my passport and looked at the photograph on the back page. I barely recognised myself in that photograph taken seven years ago, even though my appearance had not greatly changed.

I turned the pouffe to the window and across the street the playground was empty. A swing moved gently in the breeze and when I thought about it I could hear the noise that the swing was making. Below me, in the small garden patch, an old woman on her hands and knees picked stones out of the earth. It was April. The cherry blossoms were falling from the trees and the petals settled in her hair and settled pink, plum and white on the black earth. Soon the trees would be naked.

I stood up and stretched my legs. I raised up my hands and touched the ceiling. I completed twenty press-ups and twenty sit-ups without making a sound.

I sat down and closed my briefcase.

He was breaking ice in the kitchen with a steel spike.

'My mother said it was probably all the oranges I ate when I was a child.'

He tapped a front tooth to remind me.

To me he seemed so frail, so undernourished, the essence of grey. I thought that one punch in the face would probably do it, or a foot pressed firmly upon the chest.

'But I'm happy,' he said, 'by nature.'

He was the saddest man in the world.

'There's nothing wrong with happiness,' I said, yawning loudly.

'What will you do next week?'

'Next week?'

'When you leave?'

'Then I will be leaving the country,' I said. I could feel myself swell as I said it. I told him that I had been here for six months—this was, in fact, a lie—and now it was time to move on, discover a new life somewhere else.

Of course it had long ago become difficult to separate the truth from the lies, as the only person who could verify anything was myself. And sometimes everything seemed a lie and sometimes everything was the truth, and sometimes something was a lie when I believed it the truth and the truth was a lie when I meant my best.

'How interesting,' he said.

I understood he did not give a damn.

'And how do you find working from home?'

'It can be very isolating,' he said.

'I can imagine.'

'But I find the rewards often outweigh this inconvenience.'

I sipped at my drink, *shiro* on the rocks, and I leaned back in the chair, feeling the spirit flush and warm my legs and cheeks. Down there on the floor he seemed like a small, reticent child.

'You do not believe that I am content here, I think.'

'I have no reason to believe otherwise,' I replied.

'Precisely,' he conceded, and to me then looked devastated, as if, after expending all of his passion upon a single principle, he now realised that he had misunderstood the crucial point from the beginning, which I had made, quietly, a half hour prior, before the audience.

I felt that I would sleep well. And some time later it was I who proposed that we retire for the evening.

There were no rats or luminosities. In fact, I felt the peace that sometimes comes to me, as when the burden of illusion shatters into infinite possibility, as when the long, lined palm of the future closes into the tight and exploitable fist of the present.

I lay on my side in the darkness, looking towards the part of the sliding door where I knew the coloured birds to be, fixed in flight and space.

That night I worked steadily for about an hour, washing, shining, lining. I broadened my domain by a foot or so but my boldest move was the creation of an entirely new angle that ran from the sink to the fridge.

Down there, on the floor, I felt the architect of my life. Using the white vegetable chopping board as a ruler I carefully marked out points so that the lines would be perfectly straight. I moved forward, never moving into new territory until I had made it my own. I knew that all of this was reckless but these two nights had stirred an old zeal within me, and I wanted to send myself to the limit.

So I worked, composed and competent and never mindful of the sleeping other, until, in the height of darkness, on my knees in another man's kitchen, I sensed the attendance of a second. I remained extremely still, initially believing that if I did not turn around the moment might not happen. My head shrivelled slowly and descended into my scorching neck. My exposed back and shoulders seemed ready to fill the room and rupture.

When I turned around there was no one there but then I blinked and he was standing at the bedroom door. From his room a little light strayed along his shoulder. And we gaped at each other like two staggered beasts in the forest.

The essential thing was to say something, anything, but this obligation thickened the air, drinking my oxygen, my words. My mouth fell uselessly open and I raised a silent hand, as if in salutation.

In response he raised his eyebrows high. Still on the floor I coughed to release myself from the paralysis of voice and legs and raised arm, but what emerged was nothing more than a painful wheeze that dispersed miserably in the air between us. Tears of shame and frustration began to pool in my eyes.

And with this he withdrew, two small steps taken backwards, the door pulled soundlessly across.

I slumped to the floor in suffering. After everything, it was in fact I who was the wretched actor. I had given my all to the auditorium, to the point of collapsing at the remarkable culmination, only to be repaid in silence. I longed for my pillow in the room beyond, the charming *tatami* and the white sheet pulled over my body while the night fell in through the mosquito-mesh. But after a spell, as the coolness of the wooden floor tempered my misery, and the four humours spun once more in approximate balance, I felt a coolness within myself, and a surgical foreknowledge returned my body and mind as one.

I worked until dawn. Scrambling about the floor I claimed the stove and the kitchen chair, the shower and the bathroom for myself alone, leaving him nothing but a narrow pathway that led from his bedroom to the front door. Sometimes the fear and the fury rose together, and again I was up in the high place, looking down at the other sprawled below on the floor like a bug, and then my arms worked all the faster.

As the pale morning light climbed in the window our new home was revealed. I sat on the kitchen chair, contented, toying with a paw-marked knife.

He emerged from his room shortly before seven, like the small and nervous animal does upon the yellow plain. And he dragged his computer back into his cave without looking up.

I fixed myself eggs and cheese, while listening to the tapping of the woodpecker. The coffee was strong and taken black, and with pleasure I read a few chapters, at random, from my book.

At noon he crept alongside the wall and stood by the entrance to the bathroom.

'I would like to have a shower,' he said, twisting his fingers.

I regarded him indifferently, waiting a moment for the question to settle.

'I am afraid that that is not possible today,' I said.

Then I stood up. I remember I felt tall then, as strong as a trunk of tree.

'What do you think you are doing?' he cried, and just for a moment I thought that he might weep.

'Get out, you bollocks!' I roared, shaking my fist at both him and the door.

To my astonishment I thought I saw him smile, as if in appreciation of the spectacle. He shot me a timid glare and hastened out the front door, closing it behind him gently.

In the kitchen I remained standing tall, the centre of a fading echo.

***

And then the days passed strangely. Eight days to be precise.

I soon commandeered most of his room and personal possessions. He transcribed passages from small notebooks while I wandered about the apartment. I fingered through a shoebox of old letters without finding anything of interest. It was difficult to finish anything. I listened to CDs and did my workouts. I prepared food and stood on the balcony staring out over a city that did not, any longer, appear so grey and uniform. In a sense I began to forget that he was there at all. We seldom spoke.

In this new beginning I was an awkward creature rambling mutely from room to room, almost afraid to touch and take pleasure in the objects I had won. Everything seemed an illusion. I carefully folded towels and sorted knives from forks from chopsticks. A number of times I cleaned the kitchen window with a damp rag. I regularly swept out the area for shoes by the door. And I took special care with the green potted plant, allowing what I judged to be the right amount of water and sunlight each day.

These minor triumphs improved me and I relaxed somewhat in my approach to the game. Of course, everything *was* a game. But I could not remember if there were rules or rights or if there was a limit. I did not know what people could accept or what I should expect of myself. The battle had been exhilarating. But now, triumphant, I couldn't even remember what had prompted me to do anything in the first place. Sometimes I would find him staring at me from his immobile position in his room.And I began to feel sick inside, as if my soul was turning.

On the sixth morning I made breakfast. Eggs with ham and cheese and tomato. Fresh bread and coffee. I brought him a plate, which he accepted without a word.

I spent the rest of the morning cleaning away the white lines on the floor. Although the chalk had already disappeared in many places, he had never strayed beyond the border and remained reluctant to leave his room. I confined myself to my own room and the balcony for more than a day before he ventured out into the kitchen proper.

He was pale and hushed and walked slowly to the sink. He fixed himself some coffee and sat at the kitchen table with his elbows guarding the cup and his chin resting upon his coupled hands. He sat like that for some time as the steam from the coffee rose about him, staring straight ahead at a point on the naked wall. Just then I thought that he, too, understood nothing. That evening he accepted my offer to fix him a drink. I selected a triangular piece of ice and watched the spirit smooth its edges.

We still seldom spoke, and typically it was he who would address me, requesting a particular food from the market, concerned about the cleanliness of the apartment, never mentioning what had gone before.

And he smiled from time to time, a gesture that never failed to lift me. We were almost a regular couple. I watched children playing in the park and I was saddened when the last pink blossom fell from the last blooming *sakura*.

At nightfall it became my habit to watch the sun set behind the mountain. It no longer spoke to me, calling me west, but was simply fine-looking and pure. And now and then, during the day, I would stand upon the other balcony and observe the city, watching for changes out there as the shadows fell. I believe I may have begun to understand that much was happening in the world, and that much was beyond my control.

***

After crossing the railway track I walked for ten minutes without noting the direction. I was wearing his casual dinner jacket, loafers, and my own tan trousers, recently pressed and cleaned. Up above, bright fat clouds hurried the sun across the sky but the day was fine and a warm and easy breeze blew through the laneways, carrying the scent of the onrushing evening.

I bought a drink at one of the machines and drank it sitting on a small stone bridge in a public garden. Around the garden, on small pedestals, were worn, stone icons of Buddhism. I noticed the black ceramic cats in bush-sheltered groves. People left change between the paws, hoping it would bring them good luck.

The long branches of two large trees stretched out and over me, holding everything together. In the clear water of the stream and garden pond, the leaves and the fallen flowers had come to each other in various clumps by the bank. Soon they would move on, washed up or taken back or torn apart. I left some coin between a cat's legs and walked away.

In due course I found my way back to the apartment block. It stood high, rectangular and yellow, surrounded by a carpark, a playground, a house and a factory, and then everything else in its order.

After checking the mailbox I climbed the three levels of steps to apartment twenty-one. I turned the key in the lock. I removed my shoes and jacket and I stepped inside. Immediately I detected the vile smell of tobacco. Then I saw that the computer had been restored to its original place on the kitchen table. Beside it, an essay-sized manuscript. From my room I heard the sounds of urgent lovemaking. Faintly nauseated, I read the cover page of the manuscript.

My name was there, I saw this right off. It was also on the next page, and, flicking through, only my surname was mentioned. It was strangely disorientating to see my name in print. What I appeared to be holding was a detailed record of my stay in the apartment.

The bedroom door pulled across. My sister stood brazenly in the gap, a white sheet wrapped tight around her waist and shoulder, a single white breast hanging towards the floor. I noted that her nipple was still hard.

She stood there, looking evenly at me, while I tried to find my voice. But I merely found myself looking at her breast. Then he appeared behind her, wearing tight-fitting, white shorts. And he was so much bigger than I had imagined.

'Well,' I said, leaving the pages back on the table, 'fancy this.'

They said nothing. I felt panic and heat behind my eyes. But not a trace of anger.

'I'm not feeling too well,' I said. 'I don't suppose we've any aspirin.'

My sister stepped barefoot into the kitchen, covering herself properly with the sheet. I remembered a tall woman with a fierce temper, but she did not come too close.

'Have you had a pleasant stay?' she asked sweetly.

As it was clear that I was struggling for an answer she motioned towards the bedroom door.

'I hope that he has been accommodating,' she said.

I looked at him. I thought momentarily that he might defend me but he wouldn't even meet my eyes and suddenly I felt truly ill, sick to my stomach and light-headed. I pulled out the kitchen chair and sat down.

'Seriously,' I said, black spots in my field of vision, 'just some medicine, a glass of water.'

Through the blur I saw the plant by his feet and wondered if it had been watered.

'No,' she said, in a considered tone of voice, 'I think it's best if you leave us now. As you can see, we're busy.'

As quickly as I had become ill, I now felt partially restored. I stood up.

'Yes,' I said, 'of course. I wouldn't want to intrude.'

'And besides,' I continued, almost as an afterthought, 'I wouldn't call this much of a family reunion.'

My sister shivered violently and stepped backwards into his arm.

'You haven't been family for a long time,' she said, quietly. 'You're not family at all.'

It was quiet and I could hear my own heartbeat. My breath came short and fast and I realised that she was crying and I immediately accepted that she was speaking the truth.

'Well, yes, of course,' I said. 'If you'll just give me a moment to gather my things.'

Neither of them said a word. I stepped past them into the *tatami* room and saw their clothes in a heap on the yellowing mats. I felt sick again. Beside the futon my briefcase was open. I removed the passport and stared impassively at my underpants, my pages, my bits and pieces. I put the passport in my jacket pocket and left the rest behind.

They had moved to the other side of the kitchen. I had not seen my sister in two years. And the more I studied this girl now the less I seemed to recognise. I recalled that my sister's hair was blonde, not brown. My sister would certainly never cry like that. And, in fact, my sister was slightly taller. Clearly this girl was telling the truth; she wasn't my sister after all. I decided that we had made a mistake, and nothing more.

Just then he bent down and picked up the plant, stepped into the room and handed it to me. I thought it a fine gesture. He went back and put his arm around the girl. I picked up the pages from the kitchen table.

'May I?' I enquired of him.

'It's yours,' he said.

I put down the plant, folded the pages and put them in my inside pocket, beside the passport.

Then I looked at them both for the last time. Her head was against his chest. It was true, we'd all of us had a shock. I thought about going across and shaking their hands. But then I thought better of it.

I put on my shoes and tied them and picked up the plant.

'I'm sorry for all this trouble,' I said.

One of them said something too but the door closed so quickly I couldn't hear a word.

Like Fish
Mick Rainsford

THE FISH HAD NO HEAD. It was the first thing we noticed when we got up close. The body was about two-foot long. With the head I reckon it would've made three.

The fish had washed up on the sand, just beyond the pull of the waves that toyed with its tail now. It was freshly killed: you could tell that right away. Its belly was the colour of Milk of Magnesia, its back mottled, grey-green and glittery still. There was no rot either. No smell of it. Just that spermy smell you get off things that live in the sea. Where the head should have been attached though was all red and chewed up and pulpy.

'The poor fish,' Johnny muttered.

I'd run into Johnny that morning. Downtown. A Sunday it was. Early. I woke around six. I was hot under my skin. The veins swelled in my temples. It felt as if some small thing with sharp feet was kneading the walls of my stomach. I tried to fall asleep again but I couldn't, so I climbed out of bed and dragged on some clean clothes and went out. I meant to get a box of Alka-Seltzer and go back to bed but the all-night mini-mart on the corner was closed and I kept walking. The town was nice at that hour anyway, before the traffic got going.

I spotted Johnny in the Spar on the main square buying a bottle of Coke. I stepped inside and grabbed a Pepsi out of the fridge and stood at the end of the queue. There were four of us in the queue: me, Johnny, a security guard with egg or something on the front of his shirt and this oulfella who handed the cashier a newspaper that was as thick as the Book of Kells.

I reached past the security guard and tapped Johnny on the shoulder. 'Tom!' He seemed really glad to see me. Overly glad. All the colour was gone from his face except for these little pink blotches here and there. There was a scratch under his right eye. He looked shook. Guilty. It made me wonder what he'd been at the night before.

Most of the night I couldn't recall myself. It had started off well enough. I remembered the first pub, Happy's, and the second. I thought I'd check out that new place, the Sarah Jane. I remembered sitting next to a crowd of yacht owners who all seemed to be enjoying themselves, remembered sneaking glances at the good-looking women in their company.

The evening ticked through the emerald and gold numerals on the big Guinness clock above the bar, through the matchstick-thin seconds, the quarter-inch minutes, the half-inch hours. The sense of promise I'd felt earlier ebbed away. I thought people were eyeing me, hunched there on my own in a cloud of cigarette smoke. I took to drinking faster. In the end I left the pub to go searching for Johnny. I hadn't seen him in weeks but all of a sudden I wanted to tie one on with my little brother.

'Where were you last night?'

'Everywhere,' Johnny said, as the cashier wiggled his bottle of Coke over the scanner. 'I don't know where I was.'

'I was looking all over for you.'

'Yeah?'

'I tried The Anchor and all.'

'I was in there for a little while all right.'

'So the barman said. We musta just missed each other.'

'Fancy a stroll?' I asked when we got outside the Spar. The phrase seemed so archaic that I grinned and added, 'old boy.' We headed towards the beach.

We uncapped our bottles and sipped as we walked. We packed in trying to talk after a while and just walked and sipped. Johnny kept lagging behind, stopping to lean against a wall or a lamppost, gasping and heaving like a stooped, pallid fish out of water. The nausea would pass and he'd catch up with me again.

Coming down the hill that leads to the harbour, the sea was suddenly there in front of us. It swelled up over that part of the town, so big and blue and clean. The ochre buildings, the red and green boats, looked mean and grimy and irregular against the broad even bay.

'Wait,' Johnny mumbled as we made the beach and I turned in time to see him lurch for the sea wall. He gripped onto two stones that jutted from the top. His head dropped, his shoulders hunched and he puked. I looked away as he shuddered and gasped. The sand which stormier days had packed against the wall covered the soles of my boots. It was almost white. Silver grains sparkled up from it here and there. Tufts of dark pointy grass poked through the sand all along the wall. The washed-salt smell of the sea was in the air all around us. Words like 'immense' and 'endless' drifted into my thoughts and I found myself wondering about other places.

'All right?' I asked when Johnny straightened up. He wiped his mouth on his sleeve and shuddered once more. 'Jesus.'

I lit a cigarette as we turned onto the beach. I fixed it between my lips and took a pull. The smoke scratched the back of my throat. It smouldered down into my chest and twisted in my guts. I flicked the cigarette at the water. It landed on the wet sand a couple of feet away. 'I'm gonna give these fuckers up,' I said. Johnny only nodded. He looked too sick to talk. I remembered an argument from the night before. At least I remembered bits of it. Outside some club. A white shirt, a dicky bow, and then the flashback was gone. I imagined myself lunging off down some poorly-lit street.

Clots of dark kelp had been left along the beach by the tide. They put me in mind of tangled eight-track tape, of those mad old yokes our father and mother used to play, those big, thick, rectangular cassettes. I remembered the music: Don Williams, Kris Kristopherson, Roger Miller. *God didn't make the little green apples, and it don't rain in Indianapolis in the summertime.* I thought about saying something about it to Johnny but he'd been so young then, he probably wouldn't remember it.

A pair of gulls wheeled and screamed way out. I caught the flashes of white as we walked, soaring, dropping, circling one another. Out there the water was grey and striped with long low waves. Rising and falling, rising and falling, the waves made the same sound as sand poured over glass. I couldn't shake the notion that the sea was watching us.

The Pepsi was working now, forcing me to burp the sick feeling from my stomach. Tiny bubbles popped in my mouth, prickling my tongue. We crunched over a Milky Way of smooth stones, our feet slipping on some, pushing others deeper into the sand. Surf rushed onto the beach in big frothy peaks before slipping back into the sea, hissing and tinkling between the pebbles and stones.

I sucked the cold air into my lungs. I imagined it working on the cigarette tar. I began to feel a bit better. Not just in my body either. I began to think that maybe I'd go easier on the drink from now on. I promised myself then that I would—I would go easier on it.

I'd help Johnny with it too. I'd start looking out for him the way an older brother is supposed to do. I watched him walk, a little ways ahead of me now, and for a second it was as if we were boys again. As if our parents were still around, somewhere close.

'I think I'll knock it on the head,' I said. 'For a while anyway.'

'What?'

'The drink.'

'Me and all.'

There was another flashback. 'Tuam,' said a face I couldn't recall—I must've asked the face where it came from. I remembered the darkening evening in the big frosted window behind the face. I remembered, after I was told where, nodding and saying, 'Galway.'

'Tuam,' the face said, 'used to be a good town to claim you were from. Now I'm ashamed to say I come from there.'

'How's that?'

'Ever heard of the Saw Doctors?'

I started to laugh.

'What?' Johnny asked.

And you know when you're feeling as bad we were feeling right then? Kind of hoping, kind of searching for something to lift you? Well, that's the way he asked me. I mean you could hear that hope in his voice when he asked.

I was about to let him in on it when we spotted the fish. We thought it was a plastic bag at first, before we realised it was something dead. Reluctantly we made our way over to it.

'The poor fish,' Johnny muttered as we stood staring at it.

'I think it's a dogfish,' I said to force down the rush of depression his words had released in me. Johnny grinned weakly, 'He musta run into a rottweiler-fish then.' I grinned weakly in reply. It was a pretty stupid joke, I know, but we needed it.

I touched the belly with the toe of my boot. The whole body wobbled. Shivered. Slimy green stuff oozed out of this little slit near its tail. 'Ugh!' Johnny made a face and turned his head.

'Probably got caught in a propeller,' I said.

'Poor bastard,' said Johnny, shaking his head slowly and I started to feel lousy all over again. Behind us was the steady, scraping, hiss-hush of the sea.

The gulls screamed again. They were closer now. They'd find the fish soon. Then more gulls would come.

'Will we head back?' Johnny nodded.

We turned around and began to walk back towards the harbour.

'I never seen a dogfish before,' Johnny said, glancing over his shoulder. 'They're some sort of shark, aren't they?'

'Yeah,' I said.

'I'd like to have seen it with its head on.'

I didn't say anything. I was thinking about this tourist place I knew up in the harbour. I got on well with the owner. I was pretty sure he'd let us in if we knocked on the side door.

Your Star Is In The Ascendancy

Kathleen Murray

'WHAT DO YOU DO DURING THE DAY?' Eddie asked me when he got in from work, while he was watching the news.

I knew he was going to ask that. I had been lying on the couch under a blanket and had set the alarm to get up an hour before he came home. Now we were both sitting on the couch, the blanket was back on the bed. A few years previous, when I had been on extended leave, Jim, my old boyfriend, came out with the same question. Jim was curious about things, whereas Eddie is careful. Eddie asked me questions maybe twenty-four hours after they first came into his mind. I could see when the question was forming and usually a day later he would ask it, in a neutral tone when we were watching the news or one of our TV series. That's because he is a thoughtful guy. You could rehearse so many answers between Eddie thinking of his question and asking. To amuse myself I would imagine him in some other historical time, as a gladiator or wearing a Nazi uniform or just ten years back before we met, asking the same question. Whole movies played through my mind revolving around his yet-to-be asked questions.

When Jim had asked me, I said 'what do you think?' back to him, not in an aggressive way, more interested. He said, 'When I was unemployed after I left college, I'd go downtown and just join a line. Like in the post office or the bank. When I'd get to the top I'd drop out. Even a line for tickets. Once I was in a line for an audition for a TV programme. All the other kids had guitars and were stretching and doing voice exercises. I said I was a ventriloquist. It was fun, kind of social. Even if the line was slow, it kept up some momentum, always moving, always getting closer to the top and we were all in it together.'

That was the first time he told me that story and I remember because it was such a hot evening, we had the windows open. There were kids practising their dance moves outside, and I could hear them singing, doing the choruses over and over. In fact, I remember every detail about that evening for no particular reason; I guess I was in love. Jim was waiting for Senan to arrive to watch the match. His friend Senan called around every week; they were friends since school. Senan would always say to me in a squeaky voice, 'Jiminy Cricket may only be a half-inch tall but he's quirky as hell.'

They had a whole stock of catchphrases they traded back and forth in place of conversation. Jim wasn't a half-inch tall but he was shorter than Senan and a little shorter than me and I didn't mention the fact much. Jim and Senan had spent a summer in Boston together as students and those couple of months had changed their language; it was the basis for a whole host of catchphrases—*Catch ya later bud, hot tamale, Alright already*. Jim still used American words like line and sidewalk.

When I rang the home the nurse on duty didn't seem to know my mother or where she might be. It was four o'clock so I asked her to check the chiropodist or the music nostalgia club. When I got transferred through, my mother says, 'Why are you calling during the day? You at home? I can hear the radio. You should be at school.'

It had taken a year and a few minor accidents to see through the smoke and mirrors but now her senility was clear to me. Once the doctor confirmed it, I phoned Louis and laid out the situation. We were her only family and we had to be practical.

'I'm on holidays from work,' I said.

She sucked her teeth. 'Those kids next door. The way they treat that cat. Like a little Persian princess. When I passed the front window, I saw with my own eyes, it had a chair, sitting up on cushions at the table, right between the twins. It spits at me when I walk by. To be spat at on your own street.'

'The cat's gone, Mother.'

'Those twins are hussies. When we moved here first, your father offers the hand of friendship. He sees them running for school he says "shake a leg there." One says "why don't you shake a leg or maybe you want to shake my leg?" And you know what the other one says?'

'Yes I do know. She said "we usually shake hands in our country."'

'Don't mock, your father is a decent man.'

Mother's senility was like a pair of inverted binoculars in her head. All the memories after my father left are gone, her trips to Louis in New York obliterated, the four other houses we lived in vanished, her gardening columns in the local paper like invisible ink. All she thinks of is the family who lived next door to us for three years, thirty-odd years back.

'When I looked over the back wall, I saw the twins in the dirt, one of them doing her business in the yard.'

'Mother,' I said, 'they were three.'

'Three?' I could hear her frowning down the line, sucking her lips. 'They were two, they were twins.'

'No. I mean they were three years old when they did the business in the yard. They were just little children.'

Her doubts cleared and she continued. 'I went straight in and I said to their mother, "the twin is doing her business in the yard." "Which one?" she said to me. Never an invitation to cross her threshold. Who can tell them apart? And the older boy is trouble with a capital T. With his bikes and his carts.'

'You know he died, Mother. He was a bank manager, he died in a robbery. He died of a heart attack.'

Not long after Jim left, I met the older boy Thomas at a bank function I attended with a friend. Over the course of a couple of drinks, we worked out that we had both lived in the same neighbourhood, next door on the same street. I was too young to remember, so I just had my mother's stories; he had his own memories of those years, none featured my household. We slept together that night and during his Wednesday lunch breaks.

That first night together I closed my eyes and imagined he was the wild boy next door, brooding, with bikes and long hair but it was too much of a stretch. I wanted trouble with a capital T but got boring with a capital B. He was married with two kids, not twins. That summer he went on a holiday to Portugal with his family for three weeks and we didn't see each other after he came back. I heard through a friend he had the heart attack. There had been a spate of bank robberies around that time, paramilitaries. He confronted the robbers but his heart gave out just as he went for them. Turns out they were drug addicts with toy guns. The bank has some kind of memorial for him, a golf trophy. I didn't attend the funeral. I wanted to go, to see the twins grown up but I didn't want to see his boys. The twins still looked like each other. I knew because he had a fold-down wallet with pictures of his boys, his wife, the twins and their families, even his dogs. I asked him about the Persian cat but he didn't remember owning a cat. Maybe they fed strays sometimes, he said.

'The twins still look the same, Mother. They're grown up, both teachers.'

'What twins? Your father was a good man. His brother turned his head. His stories of wrapping diamonds around all the aristocratic necks of London. Telling your father that he was wasting his days with dead foxes and mink, coming home with the smell of death on his hands. I know what I would have wrapped around his neck, a noose.'

The fox, the diamonds, the noose—again, the magical binoculars were cutting out the edges, erasing details surrounding the picture. I was wearing a small, silver necklace when we had this conversation and I moved across the hall to stand in front of the mirror. I didn't stop listening but I removed the necklace with one hand and kept the phone to my ear with the other. I wanted clear space to visualise some diamonds around my own neck. If I came into a little settlement of sorts, I might even stretch to a necklace and earring set.

'If I see Lindburgh flying over this building, so help me, God, but I'll drag him from the sky with my bare hands.'

'Well, Mother, Lindburgh hasn't taken his plane up in a while but why don't you get the nurse to put your chair up beside the window so you can keep watch. And I'll be over to see you this weekend.'

*

When Eddie asked me what I did during the day what he really wanted to know was where I went if I left the house. He wouldn't like to bump in to me during his working day. It would be like a mistake happening to him and he avoided mistakes.

'I do housework and jobs mostly. If I go into town, I go to galleries,' I answered. But I did leave the house sometimes with no particular place to go because I missed the journey to and from the office, particularly the morning walk down the quays. Walking to work took me away from the city whilst most of the foot traffic was moving in the opposite direction. I was on nodding terms with a couple of fellow pedestrians. An older couple taking up the whole path, he always on the kerbside. The jogger with boyish face and hair who I recognised from growing up, maybe from a youth club or school. What are you doing with yourself if you're out jogging every day, I thought. The Spanish girl always late. She passed me by most mornings, long strands of hair sticking out at odd angles, usually in sandals and cotton patterned swing coat. I could tell how late she was depending on where our paths crossed.

As a matter of course, when I worked, I would choose my clothes based on the 7.55 am weather report, having also considered my options the night before in relation to the 11.15 pm report. Eddie enjoyed listening to the weather with me. For me the forecast drew me into myself, my body, my wardrobe, my day ahead. I could draw accurate conclusions about the next day's weather from the shipping reports at night but I still listened to the morning news just in case.

My first meeting with the union official went okay apart from his clothes. He wore an open-necked checked shirt with casual pants and introduced himself as Michael. In my previous dealings with the union, I had been assigned a more senior representative, Anthony, a suit and tie man, very sympathetic to my situation.

I told Michael the ins and out of what had happened. 'I deserve my dignity at work,' I said. 'I don't put in or out on anyone and I deserve my dignity in return.' I finished with: 'At the end of the day, she's a boozehound, and I can't be managed by a boozehound.'

I could see he was not familiar with the term boozehound but I used it to describe the boss to Eddie and it got the reaction she deserved. According to my mother you could tell by the nose if a person was a boozehound. She said we had washed up on the shores of Boozehound Island, thanks to my father.

'Well, the picture you paint is not a pretty one,' Michael said taking careful notes. 'I'm aware from your file you've moved departments before, so presumably you wish to remain in your current position. I'll stake my reputation on your reinstatement and a full and satisfactory resolution of the situation, with your dignity restored.'

I didn't know what his reputation was worth but I knew my rights. On the way home I thought that my case would make a good afternoon series. Michael was more like a character from an evening courtroom drama, a little bit too serious and long-winded for afternoons. He called the very next day and had secured three weeks special leave for me. But I already had an appointment with the doctor to renew my certificate and I had planned my lunch around it so I went down to the clinic anyway.

In the waiting room I sat between a mother with a sneezing baby and a young man, the jogger. In the surgery, in his regular clothes, he looked employed, wearing cords and a cord jacket, similar to a professor. That would explain his flexible schedule. Who wants to meet in a doctor's surgery? It could generate any kind of conversation. I picked up the first magazine from the pile—*Caravan Monthly*. Scanning the ads for second-hand trailers, hoists, tents, I hit the contact section. People, it appeared, were looking for very specific contacts to do specific things together in a caravan.

'I know you?' he said.

I tried to force a surprised smile and said, 'No, I can't quite place…' I'm not good at hiding the truth. Jessica, the new administrator, told me that, barely a week after she started. 'It's written all over your face,' she said, 'so don't bother putting on the sugary voice.' That's what I had to put up with.

'I knew your brother. How is he doing?'

One of Louis's exes. I misheard, thought he said who is he doing and was about to answer. The doctor's secretary called his name right then and he said goodbye to me and that we should meet for a coffee sometime if I'm free during the day and that he hoped I would be okay, medically.

A woman phoned me to come in for the second meeting. My union man, Michael, didn't seem senior enough to have a secretary. Maybe she was the receptionist and he just asked her to make the call.

'Amidst claim and counterclaim the waters can become muddied, very muddied indeed. A number of factors are working for you and a number against you,' he said.

I liked him less this time. Mentally, I moved him from an evening legal drama to a history channel. The folder of extra documentary evidence I had put together, notes of conversations, letters, photocopies of the boozehound's diary, were sitting over to one side of the desk, unopened and he hadn't taken the top off his pen.

'Your absences for one thing,' he continued.

'Stress related. My dignity was shattered. Everyone knows there are physical manifestations.'

'But 86 sick days in seven months and yet you clocked up 105 overtime hours in the same period?'

'Some people would see that as commitment.'

He was not meeting my eyes. 'But,' he said, his face clearing, 'management were clearly negligent in the supervision of the situation. Other staff members have corroborated some of the drink-related incidents you report. But there are also some serious allegations around bullying behaviour on your part, which as I have said previously, muddied the water. Considerably.'

Clearly he was out of his depth in this muddy water.

'I've weathered this kind of accusation before. Why am I persecuted for no reason?'

My leave was extended by another week. I had to consider the factors. That night Eddie and I watched a quiz show. But I couldn't concentrate because inside my head Michael's final phrase stuck in my mind like a jingle from an ad. It played on a continuous loop—*Your star, I'm afraid, is not in the ascendant.* Actually what Michael had said was 'your star, I'm afraid, is not in the ascendancy.' Because of his mistake I liked him less. I noticed mistakes. Even from a distance I can spot a spelling mistake. Things on food boards, shop signs, taxis, mistakes everywhere. There was a euro sign at the end of the price of soup outside a pub. When I told the waitress she said, 'I'm Australian, that's how we do it.' I felt like saying, well you're here now. But I left it. In the material shop, buying curtain tape to fix up the curtains Mother gave me from the old house, I saw across the road in the sandwich shop *Two Roles For The Price Of One.* On my way to the bus stop, I told the woman; she said, the last thing I needed was two rolls.

In the evenings I would tell Eddie the mistakes they made in work. Mostly spellings, but if Boozehound had one too many at lunchtime she could come out with anything. I kept notes in my diary. Eddie, he says, 'Go easy on those secretaries at work. They need to learn.' Or, 'Everyone makes mistakes—its doesn't mean they're bad people.' If Eddie is having an affair and I believe he is, he'll make a mistake and I'll be right on it. He knows it too. I could see him thinking for nearly two days before he asked me 'Can't you just get along and live with mistakes?' He thinks I'm not doing myself any favours but I've got to play the hand I'm dealt. Maybe he'll want to get me the earrings if I ask him and I could buy the necklace myself.

My star was not in the ascendant. Without much science behind you, who can really get a grip on the heavens? You know a star is dead before its light reaches us. Dead in the water before the lights go out. Once your star begins its descent, take it as a message you were a goner a long while back.

I can't remember when Jim's star was in the ascendant but I know exactly when it began its descent. One night, we were at a party, a work party. I was across the room but I knew by his hand movements he was telling the story about joining the queues to a group of people. Later when we got home, he smoked half a joint before we went to bed. With his head in the crook of my arm he said, 'You know what I love? Sorting out fresh laundry together, you know matching socks, folding stuff, the whatever, the smell. It's got all the rightness just doing that. Together, you know. It's love, right?'

But just once ever had he helped me fold the laundry. He happened to be in the utility room because he was stoned and found the sound of the dryer comforting. That night in bed I saw that Jim would pick one incident and make it stretch over a lifetime. The joining-the-lines story was probably just a once-off thing that had happened. Jim would use the minor anecdotes of his life like a join-the-dots picture. Living off the dots, stretching them, joining them with shaky lines to form an outline of himself. Like trying to make a plough out of seven dots of light. His star was not in the ascendant. And he fell asleep before we had sex. He was a not a join-the-lines man, he was a join-the-dots man. That was my catchphrase for him. His star was plummeting.

To me, my life seemed seamless, without a defined pattern. For example, I couldn't pinpoint the exact day when it all changed at work. Like untangling a ball of string, now I had to hold on to the end and work backwards from there. At night I would wake up suddenly and have paranoid thoughts.

'Eddie,' I would say, 'what about if I left food in the fridge and it went off and someone else had to clean it out or maybe Jeanette's scarf that went missing last December, maybe she thinks I stole it. The Boozehound knows I'm on to her and she set the dogs on me. She knows I have her number.' Or 'Eddie, what if someone with my name committed a crime? I should go to the library, the internet, look for people with the same name that would cause people to take against me.'

Eddie was the best sleeper I ever slept with. He would answer you like it was the middle of the day but in two minutes his breathing was so regular and peaceful you knew he was gone again. In the back of my mind I thought maybe the trouble was because of my family. It never came up in the office but the Human Resources Manager compiled a list at the beginning of each year for emergency purposes—next of kin, number to call in case of emergency, religion. I had ticked *no religion* but I put my mother's name as next of kin, maybe that was the giveaway, the Jewishness of her name.

The day before I returned to work the phone rang.

'Are they feeding you in that boarding school? Your father worked his fingers to the bone to keep you there.'

'I would have rung you, Mother. I have a new job now. I got a parallel promotion. I'm starting in a new section tomorrow.'

'In my day it was up or down or out on your ear. No parallel parking on the job. My boy Louis was promoted from the 43rd to the 57th floor. He's practically a part of the New York skyline, his head is so close to the clouds.'

Her memories of me had fixed now on my secondary school years, but were running a separate loop for Louis. For Louis it was the broker years, after he emigrated, the young man in a striped shirt, bringing her up to the top floor of the skyscraper, greeting colleagues in the lift. She saw his move up the building as a promotion, with the higher floors the epitome of success. He never told her he had left the firm and set up a catering company with Eric, his boyfriend. They had a place that sold high-end juices, wraps and low-fat pastries.

'Why did your father pick this hellhole for us? You know why? For the one simple reason.'

I said, 'I know already why we're here, Mother,' to try to stop her, but I had just put on nail polish so I had to sit still anyway. 'Some soldier after the war, right?'

'He was in a bar after the war. He thought the boy was Scottish but he turned out Irish. And this soldier tells your father about Lindburgh flying across the Atlantic on his solo run. And Lindburgh's surrounded by fog and he sees some little fishing boats. So he knows he's near Europe and he wants directions. So he flies down low, shouts the question, tries to get them to point him in the right direction. But they ignore him. Which direction Ireland? England? France? Nothing. They watch the man in the plane but at the same time they keep pulling up their nets and emptying them. The man in the bar told your father that not only did the Irish fishermen not help him, they didn't even bother to point him in the wrong direction. Lindburgh thought they couldn't understand English but that soldier said they understood alright, everyone had been reading about the flight in the paper for days. My

God, your father hated Lindburgh. And he thought, after all we had been through, he wanted to settle us in a place where people mind their own business and let history go on overhead. Your father is a fine man. He was at the top of his trade in this country, the best society people. His shop was filled with the ascendancy. His brother turned his head.'

When my father took up with my mother's sister in London there was never any confusion about whether to call her aunty or stepmother because we never spoke about her again at home. So, one way or another, someone turned his head and he never looked back.

'Don't worry, Mother, our star is in the ascendancy,' I replied. 'Any news on the twins?'

That set her off for another fifteen minutes and I got started on my toenails.

The new job is in a different section but in the same building. My first morning I couldn't decide whether to use the bus or to walk. I made my way down to the corner and paused to cross the road. A turn to the left would bring me to the bus stop; a turn to the right was the beginning of the walk. I was imagining sitting in front of the therapist and telling her my feelings about what? Trying to make a decision to cross the road and what type of transport to take? Part of the package is visiting her every two weeks for six months. The lights changed a number of times at the pedestrian crossing. The newspaper seller who has a regular spot against the wall came over and took my elbow.

'You need a hand across?'

God almighty, I thought, he thinks I'm gone blind.

'No problem,' I replied, 'I'm on my way.' I crossed. I'm on the way. I pictured myself saying that to people, new work people and maybe some of the old people in the canteen who might enquire after my health and well-being. Well, I would say if I spoke to them, I'm okay; my star is on the up and up again.

She Fed Her Heart on Fantasies

D.W. Lewis

IT WAS ONE OF THOSE NIGHTS—a hot night, a dirty night, the sort of night when you woke up with your face stuck to the pillow. The air conditioning was malfunctioning again, the apartment nowhere near the 64° Fahrenheit recommended as the optimum temperature for sleep. As if to testify to this fact Clairvoyance was awake. Turning on her side, she spooned up to Pilates. His bare skin was slick. Slotting herself around him, she reached down and pushed the button at the base of her penis. With a faint click the arterial gate opened and the organ began to tumesce. The penis graft had been a birthday present to Pilates in the autumn of '36. Clairvoyance would never forget the look on his face, how his eyes had narrowed with delight, as she'd stepped jauntily out of her knickers that first time. She pressed herself gently against her husband's lower back. He loved that. Correction, he usually loved that. On this occasion, as on too many occasions recently, he muttered and rolled onto his front. He was practically hanging off his side of the bed now.

'What's wrong?'

'I'm trying to freaking sleep.'

'Fine,' she snapped back. 'You go to sleep.'

Retreating to her side of the bed, Clairvoyance let her hand stray beneath the covers. The penis was a little small, and aesthetically it didn't really suit her body—her hips were wider than her husband's and these days, alas, her thighs heavier too. A cock with more girth would have been better, maybe an extra inch on the end. Although tempted to ask their plastic surgeon to enhance the organ, she'd denied herself—it wouldn't do to have a penis bigger than your husband's after all.

Toying with it, like she'd seen him do so many times, she remembered the excitement of the early twenties. Pilates and Clairvoyance. They had been one of the first couples to see the potential of transplant surgery—in particular, the new generation of immunosuppressive drugs, which meant that any tissue or organ could be grafted onto or sewn into the human body. Unlike some of the other publicity-seeking charlatans, they had transformed themselves for love. Clairvoyance and Pilates. From the initial swapping of minor body parts, a toe here, an ear lobe there, to his sacrifice of a testicle (grafted next to her labia) and her gift of an ovary and fallopian tube (implanted into the body cavity beneath his stomach), every operation they had undergone had been an expression of their togetherness. Several years later her remaining ovary had contracted a rare, incurable cancer and had been removed, but even that hadn't phased them. More than enough for each other, they'd never wanted children.

Then came their *pièce de résistance*, the most beautiful demonstration of love between two individuals ever attempted—a simultaneous kidney transplant. The symmetry was breathtaking. Two transplant teams, made up of four surgeons and eight theatre staff, carrying out the operation in identical operating theatres. Side by side, they'd held hands in the anaesthetic room, only letting go when the gas had begun to take hold. Pilates' kidney had proved more difficult to remove. As the surgeon had been about to lift the organ out there'd been a complication, a problem with the renal artery. Her kidney had remained outside their bodies for over an hour. The thought of that reddy-brown bean, throbbing and eager to germinate inside her lover's body, all alone in a polystyrene box full of ice, made Clairvoyance shudder. They had been the first couple in the world to exchange internal organs, their place in history assured by the time the final suture went in.

History was all very well but it wasn't much help for Clairvoyance's horny mood or her insomnia. She pushed the button to deflate her penis. As she got out of bed Pilates gave an angry grunt. She'd never known him so bad-tempered. Perhaps he was having trouble at work.

She mooched into the kitchen and poured herself a glass of milk. Her husband's briefcase was next to the fruit bowl on the table. Pushing aside a flutter of conscience, she pressed open the catches. Inside were work reports, his electronic organiser, pens, a calculator and a clear plastic folder containing newspaper clippings.

Clairvoyance slid the folder out of the briefcase. Underneath was a large colour photograph of Pilates and his team from the office. Pilates was in the centre, holding up a certificate, his secretary Jasmine on his left, the company president on his right. Everyone was grinning as if their lives depended on it. The photograph must have been taken last year, on the day Pilates had won an industry award. The team had celebrated with dinner and drinks in the evening. All the husbands and wives had gone except Clairvoyance who'd had a bad stomach. Pilates had rolled in drunk at five in the morning, shirt unbuttoned to his second navel, clutching the certificate. The mental picture made Clairvoyance smile—sometimes he acted like a big kid. Since the award he had, if anything, worked even harder. No wonder he was stressed out. They really should take a holiday, head up to the summerhouse for a week or something.

Next she turned her attention to the plastic folder. The cuttings were from twenty years ago, a time when casual organ transplantation was still a controversial subject. Clairvoyance pulled out the reports and read avidly. She'd forgotten so much. All that bigotry and hatred. The media coverage had been vitriolic, the right-wing press and church groups howling in outrage and condemning them as 'sick body-fusing freaks'. The commentators had advised their viewers and readers that 'this warped twosome' should be imprisoned without trial for daring to speak a love with no name. Even Clairvoyance had to admit that in the early days the majority were of a similar opinion, but soon hundreds, then thousands flocked to their cause. Many sent messages of support, praising the couple for their bravery. Websites and support groups flourished. Throughout, Pilates and Clairvoyance were comforted in the knowledge that all human beings courageous enough to push back boundaries had been doubted, mocked and persecuted. Ignorance was by far the most dangerous of the human conditions. Hugging the cuttings to her chest, Clairvoyance felt like a young girl again, in the first flush of love, believing—no, better than that—*knowing*, what was right and true.

The newspaper reports towards the back covered the euphoria of the thirties, the decade when accelerating developments in medicine began to offer infinite routes to a corporeal nirvana. Organs and body parts could now be grown *in vitro*, in Petri dishes, flasks and specially adapted organo-chambers, then, in a stunning advance, *in vivo* on the body of the recipient. Pre-programmed progenitor cells could be transplanted into tissue then activated. It was as easy as planting beans or peas. This was the method by which Clairvoyance's penis had been graftgrown, using cells from her husband. Recently things had come around full circle. Retro organ transplanting with original body parts was in vogue once more.

With a yawn Clairvoyance returned the folder and photo to the briefcase, wondering why on earth Pilates was digging up the past. As she snapped the catches into place, the calendar hanging up beside the fridge caught her eye. They were halfway through July. That meant next month was August and their wedding anniversary, their 25th wedding anniversary. Suddenly Clairvoyance had an inkling why Pilates had the newspaper cuttings. He was taking stock of course, but his reason for taking stock, if it was what she suspected, was so fantastic, so wonderful... Fear and joy surged through her body, and she knew, despite her tiredness, there would be no more sleep that night.

Clairvoyance spent the rest of the week preparing for their annual barbecue. All their friends, relations and Pilates' work colleagues would be coming. She liked to think that the evening was one of the highlights of the town's social calendar. It was certainly one of hers. This year, however, Pilates had not been keen.

'Not again,' he'd groaned. 'All those ghastly people.'

'They're our friends!'

She'd talked him round, she knew come the day he'd enjoy it, he always did. On Friday afternoon the caterers arrived to set up, laying out tables in the garden. On top of the white linen tablecloths they arranged a huge punch bowl, plates, cutlery tucked in pink napkins and neat rows of glasses, ready for the food and drink. There was a brief panic over a blocked nozzle on the barbecue, which was an old machine with an industrial-sized grill and roasting spit, but thankfully once the gas canister had been changed, it sparked up first time. As usual the first guests didn't arrive until 7.30, half an hour late, but the trickle of people in the hallway soon became a throng. Clairvoyance greeted them all, kissing cheeks and smiling, resplendent in a black cocktail dress, made of a shimmering material that was transparent in all the right places. Viewed in profile the subtle protuberance of her penis could be seen. Once everybody had accepted a drink and a plate of nibbles, Clairvoyance was able to relax. She soon found herself by the pool, sitting on the edge of a sun lounger, next to Pilates' secretary Jasmine. The conversation turned to transplantation, a subject the younger woman appeared fascinated by.

'I mean what does it feel like?' she gushed. 'It must be amazing.'

'Well, I suppose it *is* pretty amazing,' replied Clairvoyance, flattered by the attention. 'It feels like nothing else in the world. There's no greater expression of love or trust in another human being. The feeling is almost sublime.'

'I think I'd be too scared.'

'The first time is the worst, but once you've got over that... You support each other through it. In a funny way, the fear actually brings you closer together.'

'Wow.'

'I mean, these days people are very blasé. You have these dreadful multiple transplanters who go from one person to the next. They have any number of body parts stuck to them. I hate that! It's cheap, completely devoid of meaning.'

'It's just incredible, to actually change your appearance, to give some of yourself to somebody else, I mean, wow.' Jasmine tilted back her head and drained her glass of Chardonnay. Her bra strap had come clear of the straps of her dress. Annoyed, she flicked at her shoulder.

'The only thing I can compare it to is getting pregnant.'

'I don't really see...' began Clairvoyance.

'The way your body is totally transformed. I never would have guessed how different that could feel, something inside you that's not your own, I mean.'

Pilates loomed over them, stiffly holding out a glass of cola.

'I wanted wine.' Jasmine brushed away the drink.

'I think you've had enough,' he answered severely.

'Oh, for goodness sake, let the poor girl have a drink if she wants one. You're not at work now.'

Pilates glared at Clairvoyance. 'Fine.' He stomped off and returned with a glass of white wine. 'Here you are. You two enjoy yourselves.'

'Ignore him,' Clairvoyance said. 'He's been a real grump recently. Cheers.'

They clinked their glasses together.

'Bottoms up,' Jasmine giggled.

'Say, I love your nails. What shade is that? It goes perfectly with your dress.'

Next morning, while clearing up the bits and pieces the catering company had missed, Clairvoyance mentioned their conversation.

'I didn't know Jasmine had been pregnant.'

Pilates was at the sink, scraping charred meat from the barbecue grill. 'What makes you say that?'

'Something she said last night. I didn't follow it up.'

Pilates resumed scrubbing. 'I think she had a miscarriage a few years ago when she was going out with that basketball guy.'

'Her fiancé?'

'Yeah, I think so, she doesn't really talk about it.'

'Why did they split up?'

'I don't know. As I said, she doesn't talk about it.'

Clairvoyance crossed the kitchen and threw her arms around her husband. Her sleeves caught the top of the soap bubbles, which were flecked with black shards, but she didn't care. She was happy—last night had been a real success, everyone had enjoyed themselves.

'You know how lucky we are?' she said, resting the point of her chin in the small of Pilates' back.

'Hiring a catering company that didn't clean up properly?'

She laughed.

'Having each other.'

Pilates squirmed from his wife's grasp. He turned round and leant back, his hands gripping the edge of the sink behind him. His face contorted, the colour veering towards puce, his lips moving as if about to speak. No sound came.

'What is it?' Clairvoyance clutched at his wrist, pulling his hands away from the sink. 'Come and sit down.'

'I'm sorry Clair, I'm sorry.'

'What's the matter?'

'Just a funny turn that's all,' he gasped. 'Too much to drink last night.'

'What's brought this on?'

He slumped back on the sofa, his face now a bilious apple white.

'We're not getting any younger...'

'Go on.'

'It all seems to be slipping between my fingers. Sometimes it feels like we've changed everything and nothing.'

'What exactly do you want to change?' Clairvoyance asked coyly.

'Oh, I don't know.' He shook his head. 'Don't you feel the same?'

She smiled radiantly. 'I've never been happier. I honestly mean that. I feel that we're building up to something, to something *wonderful*.'

Pilates grunted.

'I know you're stressed but try not to worry. Whatever will be will be.'

She left him on the sofa and finished the clearing up herself. When she came to the sink the soap bubbles had long burst. Still smiling to herself, she plunged her hands into the cold greasy water, searching for the plug.

The following Wednesday, Clairvoyance played her usual round of golf in the morning then met up with friends in the clubhouse for lunch. After a few cocktails the conversation, as always, was steered onto sex, or lack of it. The only one who didn't complain about her husband's loss of libido was Ecstasy Conroy, who was happily divorced and shacked up with a 23-year-old lifeguard.

'We can't get enough of each other, ' she crowed. 'Honestly, I feel like a teenager again.'

She did have a healthy glow, Clairvoyance had to admit.

'Pilates and I were the same until a few months ago. Recently he's been blowing hot and cold. All over me one minute, then not interested, *nada*.' She paused for effect. 'Not a dicky-bird.'

The girls laughed, apart from Ecstasy Conroy who simply said: 'Oh dear.'

'You're telling me,' Clairvoyance replied. 'I'm going to explode.'

Ecstasy stirred her cocktail with a twizzle stick. 'No, I meant, oh *dear.*'

'Leave it, Ecstasy,' warned Grace Wenders. She was Clairvoyance's golfing partner, a tall woman, good off the tee but lousy around the greens.

'No, I want to hear this. What do you mean?'

'Blowing hot and cold is one of the first signs. Let me guess. I bet you that Pilates is working harder than ever before, that when he is at home he's tetchy, that he's started wearing new aftershave and taking an interest in his appearance.'

Clairvoyance was open-mouthed. 'One of the first signs of what?'

'Oh, gosh, do I have to spell it out. An affair, of course.'

Ecstasy sat back triumphant.

'That's… that's just where you're wrong.' Clairvoyance's face reddened with anger. 'I know for a fact that he has a lot on his mind at the moment. He's planning a surprise for our 25th wedding anniversary.'

'Don't you just love surprises?' Ecstasy countered drily.

'It's not just any old surprise… I think that… I think that he's going to propose a simultaneous heart transplant.'

The table erupted, all the girls shrieking and trying to speak at once.

'Are you crazy?'

'It's too dangerous.'

'You're surely not going to do it.'

'What's Pilates thinking?'

'Do you want to die?'

After the uproar had died down and lunch was finished, Clairvoyance was left on her own with Grace.

'You're going to do it aren't you?'

Clairvoyance nodded. 'If Pilates asks. The odds are much better these days, over 50% that both partners will survive. Surgical techniques are advancing all the time. Professor Hardwick is a world leader in the field. It just feels that now is the right time.'

'Well, if you're sure,' Grace gave her friend a little hug. 'Then I'm happy for you, I really am.'

'It's something that we've been heading towards all our lives, our destiny, you know?'

Never before had Clairvoyance waited so nervously for a day to arrive. Not for Father Christmas, not for her 18th birthday party, not for her wedding day. Every time she looked at the calendar she got a jolt of nervous energy and she was sleeping less than ever. She longed for the anniversary to be over and done with, for the chain of events that would crown their life together to be set in motion. More than anything she wanted to talk the operation through with Pilates. Maybe he had already booked them in for a preliminary consultation, paid a deposit at the clinic even. But she fought the temptation, not wanting to spoil the surprise. Instead, she searched online for support groups and found a website of a couple who had undergone the operation. They gave a glowing testimonial—how close the surgery had made them, how their lives had been transformed. *Check out this neat poem*, they signed off. *It's over 500 years old. Little did Sir Philip Sidney know that one day his* Song from Arcadia *would become reality!*

> *My true-love hath my heart and I have his,*
> *By just exchange one for the other given:*
> *I hold his dear, and mine he cannot miss;*
> *There never was a bargain better driven.*
> *His heart in me keeps me and him in one;*
> *My heart in him his thoughts and senses guides:*
> *He loves my heart, for once it was his own;*
> *I cherish his because in me it bides…*

Clairvoyance printed out the poem and kept it in her bedside cabinet, taking it out to read whenever she felt anxious.

On the morning of their anniversary, Clairvoyance awoke Pilates with a breakfast tray of eggs Benedict, freshly squeezed orange juice and a carnation from the garden.

'Surprise,' she cooed.

'What's this in aid of?'

'Aren't you the funny one? Happy Anniversary.'

She gave him a card and a silver Rolex she'd had engraved. *My heart forever yours.*

He thanked her gruffly. 'I'll give you your present after work.'

'Must you go in today?'

'Important presentation.' He pushed aside the tray and kissed her, a crumb of egg on his upper lip. 'I promise I'll be home early.'

As he showered, Clairvoyance slid the poem out of the drawer and read it through, although by now she knew every word.

Despite his promises, Pilates wasn't home early. In fact he was an hour late and stank of whisky. He threw the largest bunch of flowers she'd ever seen on the table—tiger lilies, roses, exotic orchids and antirrhinums.

'Happy anniversary, darling,' he bellowed, lifting her off the ground.

'Put me down, you brute,' Clairvoyance laughed. 'Put me down.'

During the meal Pilates put away a bottle and a half of wine. She'd heard of Dutch courage but this was ridiculous. If he drank any more he'd be under the table.

'Easy, darling,' she heard herself saying as he topped up his glass yet again.

'S'our anniversserary,' he slurred. 'Time for your present. Where did I put it?'

He patted the outside of his jacket ineffectually before extracting a slim envelope from an inside pocket. It must be an appointment card for the clinic, Clairvoyance thought excitedly, fingers fumbling at the seal.

'Oh.'

'Oh? Is that all you can say to a fortnight in China! You've always wanted to go.'

'Sorry, darling. It's brilliant. I just thought that…'

'You thought what?' barked Pilates.

'Nothing.' Clairvoyance glanced at the receipt stapled to the back of the tickets. 'You bought these today,' she gasped. 'The date's on the ticket. You *had* forgotten.'

Pilates snorted. 'I booked the trip ages ago, I just picked the tickets up tonight.'

She knew he was lying. 'Were you scared I might say no?'

'Scared?'

'It's a big leap I know. But I've been reading up about it. We can do it together.'

'What are you talking about?'

'The operation of course, the heart transplant.'

Pilates' face twitched from confused to sneering. 'You thought I was going to ask you to have a simultaneous heart transplant?'

Clairvoyance nodded.

Her husband's chin slumped forward onto his chest. For a moment he was silent and she thought perhaps he had passed out, but then the laughter began, quietly at first, building gradually to a howl. 'You thought… heart transplant… oh, that's a good one… might as well sign our own death warrants.'

'What did you mean then?' Clairvoyance yelled. 'All that stuff about life slipping through your fingers, about changing everything and nothing.'

All of a sudden the laughter stopped. 'I was talking about children, you silly bitch. I was talking about having children.'

An hour later Clairvoyance hunkered down in the kitchen, sweeping up the aftermath of the row. When she'd stormed out to the garden, Pilates had started on the whisky. She'd come back inside to try to talk to him, to apologise for getting it wrong, but her words had only served to re-ignite the argument. He'd been on the point of throwing his glass at the wall, changed his mind, then dropped it accidentally, then stood on a piece of glass. The idiot. The sight of his own blood had diffused the situation. Sorry, sorry, sorry, he'd repeated as she'd helped him to bed, yanking off his shirt and trousers when he got there. As she brushed the glass into a dustpan, the rage flared inside Clairvoyance once again. She felt like throwing a glass herself, she really did. Why did he have to bring up children? After all this time, and on their anniversary to boot. She'd told him to shut up, that it was too late to talk about freaking kids. They'd made that decision years ago—no regrets was part of the deal.

Towards dawn Clairvoyance got up to use the bathroom. The anger had turned sour inside her and upset her stomach. Sitting on the toilet, it suddenly came back to her where she had seen that colour, the miniscule trace of purple she had noticed on Pilates' little toenail when checking the cut on his foot. Rushing back to the bedroom, in her panic she forgot to wipe herself. His right foot was still sticking out the end of the bed. She turned on the light—no danger of him waking—and knelt down to peer at the toe. There was no doubting it. The surgeon had done a skilful job but the join was still visible. The toe did not belong to Pilates, and it certainly wasn't hers. The thin line of plum nail varnish near the top of the nail gave it away. Only a few weeks earlier she'd admired the same colour at the barbecue. The little whore had been wearing open-toed sandals and a summer dress. Jasmine. The toe belonged to Jasmine. Clairvoyance retched onto the floor. His secretary. How freaking predictable, how freaking obvious. How could she have been so stupid?

Pilates turned onto his side and scratched at the breast that squatted awkwardly in the middle of his chest. He was unable to sleep for thinking of the past. Surprisingly the breast reduction had been the most stomach-churning operation to watch. If it had been anyone but Clairvoyance under the knife he would have turned away in disgust, but as it was her body he had kept his gaze trained on the surgeon's gloved hands and tried to love the yellow streaks of fat being vacuumed from her tits. The excision of the half-formed third nipple on her right thorax had been a breeze in comparison—other people's blood had never bothered him. He let his fingers caress the breast. The nipple was smaller than his own and never changed in size, remaining the same little pair of pursed cherry lips, even when Clairvoyance had wetted it with her tongue. Physically he had felt nothing when she'd done this, mentally he had experienced the most exquisite surge of pleasure and intimacy. He knew that he would never have that sensation again, not with Jasmine who lay sleeping beside him, not with anyone.

Clairvoyance and Pilates. They had tried so hard to become part of each other, a fusion, the embodiment of the word *togetherness*, flesh become one. Pilates and Clairvoyance. They had been pioneers, discoverers of a new mode of expression. In the early days transplantation had been pure, meaningful, a magical flowering of love. Now, taken to extremes they could not have guessed at, any purity had vanished. A bitter tear leaked from the corner of Pilates' eye. Perhaps they should have known that their attempt was doomed to failure, he thought, that the end result was inevitable. Perhaps their mistake was that they had considered themselves different, better than other couples, joined irrevocably.

From Jasmine's side of the bed came the sound of gentle snoring. Heavily pregnant, she'd taken to sleeping on her back. He hadn't told her that she had been the trigger for Clairvoyance's suicide. One afternoon while out shopping Clair had seen Jasmine in the street. The younger woman had been wearing a maternity dress, the swelling of their child clearly visible. It had all been in Clair's note. *I have fed my heart on fantasies*, the note began.

As Pilates considered what his wife, for she had still been his wife, had done afterwards, tears swamped his eyes. That night she had brought his power tools, his drills, saws and hammers, from the garage into the kitchen. Benumbed with tranquillisers and alcohol, she had first scrubbed at his nipples with wire wool and bleach. Then she had sliced of his testicle and the penis graftgrown from his progenitor cells. Next she had sawn off all the fingers and toes that had once belonged to him. She'd also managed to cut out most of his eyelid and smash the tibia in her left leg. How had she been able to bear the pain? *It will be nothing compared to the pain I am feeling now*, she had written. His kidney she gave her best shot. *After all no one can say I'm a quitter*. Summoning up the last of her strength, she'd flung his tools to the floor, then, leaning back in a chair, kitchen table awash with blood, had chosen her favourite kitchen knife, the one with the smallest and sharpest blade, to make the final excision.

Notes on Contributors

David Albahari was born in 1948. A writer and translator from Serbia, he is the author of nine novels and eight collections of short stories. His books have been translated into fifteen languages. Translations into English include *Götz and Meyer* (Harvill, 2004) and *Snow Man* (Douglas & McIntyre, 2005). He moved to Calgary, Canada, in 1994, and still lives there.

Kevin Barry was born in Limerick in 1969 and currently lives in Liverpool. His short fiction has appeared in journals in Ireland, Britain and America. These include *Phoenix Best Irish Stories, The Dublin Review, The Stinging Fly, The Adirondack Review, The Subterranean Quarterly* and *PIF magazine*. He writes sketches and columns for the *Sunday Herald* in Glasgow and the *Irish Examiner* in Cork. He was shortlisted for the Davy Byrnes Irish Writing Award in 2004. A collection of his stories will be published later this year by The Stinging Fly Press.

Maria Behan, after nine years in Dublin and Belfast, has returned to her native America and currently lives in San Francisco, where she works as a freelance editor and writer. She has published short stories in Ireland and the UK, and received a Francis MacManus Award in 1997. She hopes to return to Ireland before long. And she hopes to finish her novel. She has many hopes.

Jennifer Brady has had stories published in *The Stinging Fly* and *Southword*. She was shortlisted for the Sean O'Faoláin Short Story Competition in 2003 and specially selected for the Short Short Story Competition by Dave Eggers in *The Guardian* in 2004. She has written and directed a one-act monologue, which was performed in DU Players Theatre, Trinity College, as part of New Writers' Week 2006.

David Butler teaches literature and creative writing at St Patrick's College, Carlow. His first novel, *The Last European*, was published in October 2005. He has won a number of awards for poetry, most recently the *Féile Filíochta* 2005.

Maile Chapman's stories have appeared in *The Dublin Review, Boston Review, Denver Quarterly*, and the online journal *5_trope*, among others. She has a Master of Fine Arts in Fiction from Syracuse University and is a former Fulbright Grantee in Creative Writing. She lives in County Wexford with her husband, the songwriter Darren Byrne, and is finishing a novel.

Ronan Doyle was born in County Galway. He has a BA in English and an MA in Journalism. Having lived in Japan for two years, he now teaches English in Dublin and writes fiction. His first story was recently published in *The Sunday Tribune*, earning him a place on the shortlist for the 2006/2007 Hennessy Awards.

Antonia Hart has been published in the *Momaya Annual Review* and *Incorrigibly Plural*, and longlisted for the Fish International Short Story Prize. She is currently completing an MPhil in Creative Writing at Trinity College. She also studied law, and later multimedia systems, at Trinity, and journalism at Dublin City University. She lives in Glasthule, County Dublin.

Claire Keegan is the author of *Antarctica*, a collection of stories published by Faber & Faber. It was published by Grove/Atlantic in the United States and was a *Los Angeles Times* Book of the Year. Her stories have won the William Trevor Prize, The Martin Healy Award, The Kilkenny Prize, The Olive Cook Award, The Allingham Prize, The Macaulay Fellowship and The Rooney Prize for Irish Literature. She was also a Wingate Scholar. Other stories appear in *Granta* and *The Paris Review*. Her second collection, *Walk The Blue Fields*, will be published by Faber next year. 'Dark Horses' won this year's Francis MacManus Award.

D.W. Lewis was born in 1974 and has an MA in Creative Writing from the University of East Anglia. He currently lives in Belfast where he runs the CultureNorthernIreland.org website.

Toby Litt was born in Bedfordshire, England, in 1968. His books include *Adventures in Capitalism* (1996) *Beatniks: An English Road Movie* (1997), *Corpsing* (2000), *Deadkidsongs* (2001), *Exhibitionism* (2002), *Finding Myself* (2003) and *Ghost Story* (2004). In 2003 Toby Litt was nominated by *Granta* magazine as one of the 20 Best of Young British Novelists. He lives in London and his website is www.tobylitt.com.

Róisín McDermott was born in County Down, in the shadow of the dark Mournes. She now lives in Kildare, via Eglantine Avenue, South Ken and Earls Court. She recently completed an MA in English at NUI Maynooth. 'Desire' is her first published story. Further short fiction will be included in an autumn anthology of new writing from the Irish Writers' Centre.

Martin Malone is the author of three novels. He has won the K250 International Short Story Award and RTE'S Francis MacManus Award. RTE broadcast his first radio play in November 2005 and his memoirs, *The Lebanon Diaries*, is due for publication in February 2007. He is currently preparing a collection of short stories for publication and revising a novel.

Kathleen Murray is originally from Carlow, and now lives in Dublin where she works as a social researcher. Her first stories were published last year in the anthology, *The Incredible Hides in Every House*, which resulted from a creative writing workshop given by Nuala Ní Dhomhnaill at the Irish Writers' Centre.

Nuala Ní Chonchúir is from Dublin, and lives in County Galway. Her second fiction collection, *To the World of Men, Welcome*, was recently published by Arlen House and her second poetry collection, *Tattoo*, is forthcoming. 'Xavier, 1995' is one of ten linked short stories from a just-written collection called *Ten Men*, the twin of which, *Ten Women*, she is now completing.

Philip Ó Ceallaigh has had over twenty short stories published in Ireland and abroad over the last few years and has appeared regularly in *The Stinging Fly*. He is the recipient of the 2006 Rooney Prize for Irish Literature for his debut collection, *Notes from a Turkish Whorehouse*, published by Penguin Ireland earlier this year. He lives in Bucharest.

Mary O'Donoghue grew up in County Clare and now lives in Boston. Her short stories have appeared in *The Stinging Fly, The Dublin Review*, the *Cúirt Annual, The Recorder* and *AGNI*. She has received a Hennessy/*Sunday Tribune* New Irish Writing Award for her fiction.

Aiden O'Reilly currently lives in Stoneybatter, Dubin. He studied mathematics and philosophy and has lived in Germany and Poland. His fiction has been published in *The Stinging Fly* and *The Dublin Review* and is also presented on his website, www.aidenoreilly.com.

Colin O'Sullivan is from Killarney and lives and works in Japan. His poetry and fiction have appeared internationally in magazines such as *The Shop, Dublin Quarterly, Staple New Writing, VerbSap, The Taj Mahal Review* and *Carve*. He has also been broadcast on RTE's *A Living Word*. He lives in Aomori with his wife and son.

Kevin Power is a short story writer and playwright. His play, *The Dinner Party*, was given a workshop by the Focus Theatre and produced by Clean Canvas Theatre Company in July 2005. He lives in Dublin. He has previously been published in *The Stinging Fly*.

Mick Rainsford has worked at all sorts of things and travelled fairly extensively. He has been published in *The Sunday Tribune, Cúirt, Comhar, MeThree* (USA) and *Poetry Ireland Review*. A regular contributor to Irish radio, he has been shortlisted for a PJ O'Connor Award and the Hennessy Emerging Fiction Award.

John Saul was born in Liverpool and has lived in England and elsewhere. His novel *Heron and Quin* was published by Aidan Ellis, and a collection of short stories, *The Most Serene Republic: love stories from cities*, published by Hopscotch, was well received in *Time Out*. Last year his novel, *Finistère*, also came out in paperback.

Acknowledgements

The editor would like to thank Brendan Mac Evilly and Amy Piller for helping him read through the original submissions. Along with Duncan Keegan they also assisted with copy editing the manuscript. Thanks must also go to Fergal Condon who did the typesetting and cover design.

The book's title and epigraph come from William Maxwell's introduction to the US edition of Maeve Brennan's *The Springs of Affection* (Houghton Mifflin Company, 1997). John McGahern is quoted from his interview in *Reading the Future: Irish Writers in conversation with Mike Murphy* (The Lilliput Press, 2000).

The Stinging Fly could not continue to exist without the various individuals and organisations, who give us their time, energy, goodwill and support.

We especially thank our Stinging Fly Patrons who provide us with vital financial support: Ann Barry, Denise Blake, Bruce Carolan, Edmund Condon, Frances Connolly, Keith Cullen, Helen Dempsey, Wendy Donegan, Fred Johnston, Conor Kennedy, Susan Knight, Joe Lawlor, David Lyons, Lynn Mc Grane, Maggie McLoughlin, Dan McMahon, Ama Mac Sweeney, Mary Mac Sweeney, Paddy & Moira Mac Sweeney, Finbar McLoughlin, Christine Monk, Maura O'Brien, Nessa O'Mahony, Kevin Robinson, Peter J. Pitkin, Fiona Ruff and Hugh Stancliffe.